The Legacy

(Families can be complicated)

DOROTHY TOPFER

The Legacy

First published in Australia by Dorothy Topfer 2025
www.dorothy.topfer.com

 A catalogue record for this
book is available from the
National Library of Australia

ISBN: 978-0-6451559-6-9 (pbk)
ISBN: 978-0-6451559-7-6 (ebk)

Front cover image: Koldunov (shotterstock) © 2025

Typesetting and design by Publicious Book Publishing
Published in collaboration with Publicious Book Publishing
www.publicious.com.au

Other titles by this author:

Sabine

Perfect Breaks

Past Presence

Also available on Kindle:

The Lost Spirit

Unravelling

Remembrance

The Life and Death of Gypsy Carmichael

Chapter One

2001

So very tired. Must try to stay awake.

Her body sways in response to the train's shuddering movements. Eyelids flickering, she fights against the waves of exhaustion that wash over her.

You cannot fall asleep. Not now, when we are almost there, she tells herself.

Glancing down, she rereads handwritten directions on the crumpled sheet of paper held tightly by cramping fingers. There is really no need to read these directions. They were already committed to memory. But then again, there's no harm in a refresher.

She reads:

> *Take the Canberra train from Central Station. Get off at Kings Vale Station. This station is not long after Goulburn and two stops before Canberra. One of us will meet you there. Just wait until we arrive. See you soon.*

It was a very matter of fact message from her aunt. No hint as to the character of the writer, nor any indication as to whether her arrival would be welcome or not. Perhaps that was not so surprising. What was surprising was that her aunt had agreed to this visit from an unknown niece in the first place.

It was also not surprising that she feels exhausted. Memories from the last few weeks are now a confused blur. As she struggles to stay awake in the almost deserted railway carriage, she tries to organise her thoughts, to better remember those recent events. Her mother's sudden illness and shock diagnosis of cancer had meant that her mother's care took priority over all else. It was soon clear that little could be done but make her mother comfortable in the hospice and be with her as she eased into the drug induced coma that preceded their final parting. With her nursing training, she knew there was no miracle cure, nor a happy outcome to be expected for her mother's condition. At least she had the comfort of sharing those last goodbyes and special words before the coma closed in and took her mother away from her for ever. She told herself that her mother's peaceful death should be a comfort, as so many said at the funeral soon after. She could find no solace in those words, feeling only rage at her mother's premature death, when she still had so much to live for. She struggled to grapple with the sense that her own life as she knew it, was now over. A future without her mother's presence in it was more than she could presently contemplate.

The letter her mother had left for her was of scant comfort and did not ease that all-pervading sense of loss. Handed to her after the funeral by Penny, her mother's godmother, and written in closely scribbled lines on the hospice notepaper, it read:

Ria dear,

I have given this to Penny for you to read after I am dead and buried. There is no point in being other than blunt. I am dying and dying soon.

I hate to leave you, as you have been the most important person to me and so much loved. I had hoped I would see you continue to grow into your life, to be with you as you celebrated your wins and to console you when things got hard. I feel like I have let you down, but believe me, I would be with you if I could.

My dear, never doubt my love for you. Please don't judge me, but for reasons that seemed valid at the time, I kept you away from my family, never realising that one day and way too soon, I would be leaving you on your own – well, apart from Penny – who isn't 'family' but should be.

I have left my sister's address with Penny and hope you may choose to make contact with her. If I had my time again – well, I would have already done this and mended bridges. Please tell her I am sorry and that I remember her with love.

I am dictating this to the nurse as I am having trouble writing today. I really can't say much more. I love you more than I could ever tell you. Having you in my life has been an absolute delight and the making of me.

Please Ria – go out and live your dreams. If there is an afterlife, I hope to see you again one day.

Your loving mum.

She could see that the word 'mum' had been written in her mother's own shaky handwriting, and then was followed by a row of wobbly kisses ending with a handwritten etc, etc.

When Ria read this note for the first time the tears in her eyes had distorted the crosses at the bottom of the page, so they appeared to be an army of kisses marching into infinity. Perhaps holding onto that thought of an infinite amount of love should have helped ease her pain - but somehow it didn't.

Now sitting in the rocking railway carriage, Ria ponders once again her reaction to this letter. When she had first read that letter, it had been not long after her mother's death. The funeral and wake now over, she and Penny had both collapsed on a garden bench outside in the paved courtyard behind Penny's house, sipping white wine, and contemplating the empty space in front of them. Both of them too drained to talk. Mind blank and body exhausted, it seemed to take all of Ria's energy just to sip and swallow. Ria's mind was far away, when Penny reached into her handbag and produced an envelope, which she held in front of Ria.

'Here. Take this note. You don't have to read it now. But your mother gave this to me a few weeks ago, to give to you after the funeral.'

Seeing Ria's hands staying resolutely in her lap, Penny leant across and pushed the envelope under her hand.

Penny, her weathered face gaunt with grief whilst showing concern for Ria, leant closer and wrapped an arm around Ria's shoulders.

'I can't make the pain go away, but I can share it if you will let me. Your mum was much loved by all of us. She was so full of light and laughter. It was impossible not to love her.'

Penny's voice trailed off as she stared ahead and then, taking a deep breath, she continued: 'Sure, she was my god daughter, but I didn't really get to know her until she moved in with me all those years ago. And then she had you. Such fun we had in this old house.'

Again, her voice trailed off as Penny contemplated those happy times not so long ago, when the house was full of noise, love and laughter.

Ria's fingers fiddled with the envelope, and almost, as if against her will, she found herself working at the semi-sealed flap so that it parted and surrendered its contents. She pulled out the note and started reading. With each word read, the flow of tears increased. As her tears dripped onto the paper, Penny tightened her grip on Ria's shoulders and pulled her closer.

'Your mum told me what she wanted to say in that letter. She thought it was important that you met what remains of your family. Your grandparents, whom I knew quite well, are no longer with us. I had very little contact with them for years before their death. Really from about the time your mother ran away, our contact lapsed.'

'Ran away?'

'Yes, that's right. Bianca ran away. I'm not sure what caused it and she made it very clear I was not to ask. Bianca was always a restless child, and I suppose it was no surprise life in a small rural village didn't appeal to her. Anyway, it is a long story and I will tell you what I know about it one day – but not now. I'm too exhausted after today. But just let me say that all those years ago when Bianca arrived at my front door, it was the best thing that had ever happened to me. Then your birth and the years that followed, just built on that.'

Drawing a breath Penny continued, 'I suppose I should have encouraged your mother to resume contact with her family. Maybe I didn't for my own selfish reasons, as I enjoyed having my little family to myself. But I can totally understand why your mother wanted this to happen now you are on your own, apart from me, that is. Think about it Ria dear – for your mum's sake.'

And she did. When she wasn't grappling with the processes brought into existence by the death of a loved one: the clearing out of cupboards, disposal of once loved now surplus possessions; responding to kindly meant, but distressing correspondence, and the winding up of her mother's pitiful estate. All the while in the back of her mind the refrain playing over and over:

You have an aunt and maybe even a family! Are you brave enough to meet them?

Or will you wimp out like always?

Over and over it played.

Until one day.

Enough, she said to the Greek chorus in her head. Enough. *I will do it and you will have to live with whatever consequences flow.*

With that, the refrain ceased, and she proceeded to make her arrangements.

****

The train slows. She looks up, glancing for some indication as to their current location. A sign comes into sight, in line with the carriage windows. She reads *Kings Vale* and consults her note. Yes, this is the place.

In a rush, she grabs her bags and escapes the carriage onto the railway station platform. The other people alighting bustle across the platform with purpose and with noise, quickly disappearing through the exit gate. Ria stands still, a bag held in each hand, her gaze examining her surroundings. Not that there is much to look at. A railway station built some hundred years ago in a generic railway station style. Nothing distinctive about it, and, judging by its appearance of dusty neglect, this railway station has seen better times. With the backs of the last of the passengers disappearing through the exit the platform is once more resuming its forlorn, deserted appearance.

The train slowly departs, revealing a similarly deserted platform across the tracks. As the noise of the train fades into the distance, a silence descends, and the railway station once more falls into slumber. She is reminded of a scene from a cliched western movie - a desolate space, absent of life with tumble weeds drifting down the empty street. This mental image is further reinforced as she emerges from the building out onto the street to be met by – nothing. The other passengers have long gone, and it is now as if they never were. Before her a vacant car park and a deserted street.

Despite the promise in her aunt's letter there is no one here to greet her. No taxi, no taxi rank and certainly no bus. Even if there was, she has no idea where her aunt lives. All she is certain of is the name of the farm – *Kings View* via *Kings Vale*.

Given the size of the village she ponders whether all are known to each other. Maybe, just explaining to one inhabitant that she needs to get to *Kings View* would be enough to obtain directions. Only problem is – she can see no-one.

Up and down the road are scattered a random arrangement of small weatherboard cottages. Built some time ago in the rural vernacular of that period, they sport steeply pitched corrugated iron roofs, punctuated at each side with a brick chimney. A veranda across the front and with a paddock between each cottage and its neighbour, perhaps once intended for the milking cow, but now adorned with an abundance of weeds. A warm wind blows dust in whorls up the street and she half expects to see a cowboy stride out of that dust swirl, with purpose and with hands resting on his holster.

Her head is in a whirl as she ponders her dilemma.

What have I done? What is this place? Have I arrived into an alternate universe? This is such a bad idea. When can I catch the next train home?

She sits on the edge of a paint scabbed bench; bags neatly arranged on each side and waits – and waits – and waits.

The late afternoon light is glowing a reddish pink. She has long given up looking at her watch but suspects an hour has passed since she first arrived at the station. Some distance away and down the street, she can see cars pulling up outside a two-storey building. People alighting, doors slamming and small groups amassing, then wandering into that building. A pub maybe? She decides that if no one appears to fetch her in the next half hour, she should wander down and make inquiries. If nothing else maybe she could find accommodation there for the night and catch the morning train back to Sydney. Why did she decide to come here? After all, her mother once left never returned and Ria is fast coming to wonder if perhaps there was never a good reason for her to come to this place.

Chapter Two

At some distance, the sound of a car. Its approach made known by a chorus of rattles, punctuated by an occasional high-pitched bark.

A vehicle pulls into the railway station carpark. Old, but not vintage. Dusty, battered and multi-coloured, bearing testament to a lifetime of various make do repairs. This vehicle is plainly not a thing of beauty. It is a work horse, a farm vehicle – a utility. The front bonnet protected by rail attachments that Ria recognises as a bull bar, not just to protect from bulls, but also protection from damage by collision with kangaroos, who she soon learns are a constant menace. She will also soon learn that the array of spotlights adorning the roof are for use at night when hunting or spotlighting for rabbits, foxes or kangaroos. In the back, a black and tan kelpie dog – quivering with excitement and barking non-stop.

The car slows to a halt. The car door opens and a young man alights. He is tall and muscular. In another life she might have thought him of interest, if only he wasn't so ... so ... scruffy!

Blonde hair in ringlets of various shades from sun-bleached to golden through to a pale ginger stream out from his head in wild abandon, almost as if each ringlet was tripping over the other in its effort to escape from his head. So obviously not seen by a hairdresser for months, if not years. On his face, a patchy, ginger fuzz that could or could not be an attempt at a beard or could be just further evidence of someone not into self-care.

And his clothes! Well, they certainly owe nothing to top end shops. The t-shirt fits loosely with frayed edges at the collar hanging free. The logo on the chest faded and missing some letters. She can only assume that it must be a beloved memento from a special event, a pity she can't tell what event it was.

And the jeans! Ripped and frayed, but not in the manner of those worn on Sydney streets. Splattered with mud and grease, they really are something to be avoided or consigned to the bin. Likewise, his boots – riding boots – scuffed, the side elastic stretched and worn down at the heel, they do nothing to enhance the outfit.

But as he strides towards her, Ria no longer notices the mess that is his appearance. All she can see is the welcoming smile, the blue eyes twinkling at her and the arms stretched out wide to greet her with a hug. And he does.

'Cousin Ariadne! At last. It is Ariadne, isn't it? Welcome.'

Struggling for air, she releases herself from the massive bear hug and steps back.

'Yes, it is. But please call me Ria. I only get called Ariadne when I am in trouble. That name is such a mouthful. You can only imagine the teasing I got at school. I don't know what mum was on when she called me that. Thank goodness I can shorten it to Ria!'

'Tell me about it,' he laughs. 'What was with your mum and mine and their liking of fancy names?'

'You too?' She asks, pondering what could possibly be worse than Ariadne?

'Yep. Mum called me Benedict. She chose it, not dad. I can see from your expression that you're thinking this name is ok. Well, it may be trendy now, but not here in this hick town when I was little. All the names I was called, until I got bigger and stronger and could beat them up!'

Seeing Ria's puzzled look, he elaborates.

'You know with a name like *Benedict* it's rather obvious – no creative intelligence required. *Dickface*, *Dickhead* and so on. Kids can be so inventive – not! But you can call me Ben. That's what everyone calls me these days.'

He leans forward and grabs her bags, tossing them into the back of the truck, just missing the dog, who is straining at her chain, trying also to welcome Ria in her own special way.

'Don't mind her. That's Bess. She just loves company – a friend to everyone. She helps me on the farm. Does more work than me, don't you, old girl?' he says patting the quivering dog on the head and in turn, receiving an adoring lick.

'Come on. Hop in. Let's get you home. I'm in trouble already, for forgetting to pick you up. Don't want to make it even worse by getting you home even later!'

It doesn't take them long to leave the village. Laid out in the grid arrangement beloved of so many country towns and bisected by the railway line, it really is only four or five blocks until they reach the outskirts. The road then passes through level farmland on which sleek cattle and shorn sheep graze. They progress this way for some few minutes before taking a left hand turn off the bitumen onto a rutted dirt road that slopes upwards heading to a scrubby hill.

'Steady now. This gets a bit rough you know. Dirt road and all that. Gets a bit of traffic and not much maintenance. In some parts, there are more potholes than road – see just like this bit!' He laughs as the car lurches, not fussed at all by his head banging on the car roof when they hit a particularly lethal pothole.

Ria hangs onto the arm strap as she is jolted to and fro, up and down and wonders how much more of this she can take. The view out the window has changed as the road climbs the hill. They are now surrounded by straggly gum trees that compete with each other for whatever sustenance the gravelly soil provides. Underneath spiky grasses grow.

Once they reach the crest of the hill and start the descent, the trees thin out. The spiky grass disappears and is replaced by lush pasture.

Ben slows and then stops the car. Lower down and laid out before them a valley, and behind that another line of tree covered hills. He points at a row of trees in the valley which run along a gash in the landscape, beside what Ria can only assume from this distance is a creek. Behind those trees she can see a curved driveway veering to the left off the road and beyond that a cluster of buildings, largely obscured by towering trees.

'There. That's home,' says Ben, the pride in his voice clearly discernible. So much so that Ria feels obliged to respond. She understands an admiring comment is required.

'Wow! All this is your home? That's amazing.'

'Yep, it's a big farm arright. Our land takes up all this valley.' He sweeps his arm around. 'Most of the farm buildings, the sheep yards, shearing shed, and that sort of thing are over there.' The arm travels to the right. 'They're all across the road. Now this here.' Arm now travelling left. 'This here is the main house and just to the side of it. There.' arm travelling further left, 'are some of the farm cottages which were all once occupied by the people who worked on the farm. These days only one is still used by a farm worker. The other three – well, I think you and Shelley, who is Mum's assistant, are sleeping out in one, Norma, our retired housekeeper, is in another. We keep one for use by guests attending functions at our place – usually used by the happy newlyweds.'

Ria, open mouthed, takes in the scene before her. It really is a spectacular view with the hills on the other side of the valley glowing pink in the late afternoon light. The trees by the creek, poplars she thinks, stand straight as pillars and are showing signs of an early autumn golden blush. Cattle and sheep are scattered across the various paddocks in the valley. So much space and such a feeling of peace.

All her life Ria has lived in inner-city Sydney and has taken her cramped surroundings for granted. Now with this expanse of nature spread out before her she can feel herself expanding, each breath deepening as she relaxes into this open environment, so much larger than anything she has ever experienced.

The car moves on and they commence the descent into the valley. Clattering over the single-lane wooden bridge that crosses a weedy creek, they turn left through a gateway, jolt over a cattle grid and then traverse a sheep filled paddock. The sheep in their path scatter in all directions.

'Don't worry about them. I have to move them tomorrow. Or maybe I should move them now. I think mum wants them out of the way before the open day.'

'Open day?'

'Yeah. Mum does it once a year. The local garden club uses the opportunity as a fund raiser and mum sees it as a good way of promoting our place for her event business. You know as a venue for weddings, birthdays and that sort of thing. People like it here,' he says complacently as he grins across at Ria.

'I think I might have arrived at a bad time then. Won't I be in the way?'

'Not at all. It's a good thing you're here. You can help mum tomorrow. Sure, she has Shelley, but another pair of hands will be welcome. You'll see. It gets pretty crazy on these open days. Once a year is about all I can bear,' said with a grimace and a laugh.

More bouncing, as they bump over another grid beside a gate on which an ornate sign proclaims, *Kings View* in black gothic style lettering. The driveway continues, but this time it is clear they have entered a garden – and a grand one at that. Tall trees, oaks she thinks, line the driveway. Underneath these trees are plantings of glossy evergreen bushes. Before them a house emerges. More like a mansion than a house. The drive curves to the left and ends with a circular driveway in front of an ornate two storey entrance.

Ben brings the car to a halt out the front.

'This is it - home. I'll take your bags down to your cottage in a little while. First though I'll take you inside to meet mum. You can have a chat with mum and Shelley, while Bess and I sort out these sheep. There's a side door we use every day, but as it is your first time here we'll do it properly, and enter by the front door. Come on!'

With that Ben leaps out of the car and gestures for Ria to follow. Climbing carefully down from the vehicle Ria stands still, stretching, arms clasped above her head and then slowly looks around. The sense of unreality that has been her companion all day remains, and, if anything, increases in its impact.

Is this for real? she wonders. *Or have I strayed onto the set of some historical drama? A sort of Australian Downton Abbey?*

In front of her an imposing residence built of stone in varying shades of sand, tan and grey, with the windows edged in red brick. The entry is double storeyed and towers over her, as if to emphasise the insignificance of anyone entering its portals. To the left a single storey extension punctuated by large windows, around which climbing roses display fragrant pink and peach blooms. Behind her and to the sides of the building are massed plantings of trees and bushes, which have the effect of screening the road from view. The hush of the garden echoes her own held breath, as she takes in all the grandeur that surrounds her. Then, a distant screech of cockatoos breaks the silence.

'This way Ria,' Ben calls from the entrance where he is standing, clearly impatient for her to follow. 'Come on, I'll take you into the kitchen where mum should be. Then I'd better go and finish my chores before dark.'

Ria follows him through massive ornate wooden double doors that Ben leaves ajar. Before her an entry foyer with worn stone slabs underfoot. To her right a marble topped table, on which is set a massed arrangement of roses in shades of red, yellow and orange. Their fragrance rises to greet her as she brushes past.

Following Ben down a corridor she takes curious glances around her. The corridor, more an enclosed veranda, has clear windows out to her left onto a large stone paved courtyard. In the centre, towers a tree of venerable age. A scattering of chairs and benches are indications of frequent use. But not by her as Ben, still talking, urges her on.

'I'll show you around later, but for now I have to rush. In here – this way to the kitchen.' He opens a door to the right and gestures her in.

Chapter Three

They walk into the largest kitchen Ria has ever seen. Built for a time when such a kitchen would have been a bustle with domestic servants. It is enormous. By the window a double sink looking out onto more gardens – vegetable gardens, she suspects, and further out a vista of lawn, a tennis court and a swimming pool.

Within an enormous chimney alcove is an Aga, that radiates a gentle heat. Even on this late summer night the room has a slight chill feel and the warmth is welcome. A small fluffy white dog snuggled in a basket by the Aga looks up as the door opens. Ria's arrival is immediately dismissed as being of no interest and the small dog resumes its slumber.

An ancient dresser dripping with blue and white crockery resides to the left of the door and in pride of place in the centre of the room rests a massive table made of well-scrubbed pine. A table that must have been in the same location for generations, for with its size and weight it would have been impossible to move. At the table two women stand side by side, deeply focussed on their work. The younger woman carefully joining biscuits together with icing, while the older woman is intent on mixing something in a very large bowl.

Already Ria knows that this older woman must be her aunt as evidenced by her close resemblance to her mother. The same reddish blonde hair – possibly shoulder length – but today pulled back tightly into a ponytail. Pale skin – freckly and slightly weather worn. Eyes like a summer's day, now glancing up at the noise of the door opening.

'Oh, it's you. Here at last. Welcome Ariadne. No time to talk. We need your help. Just put your coat somewhere and give Shelley a hand icing those biscuits. I have to get this mixture into the oven and then we can catch up.'

Those eyes now focus on Ben and she continues.

'Ben, you've forgotten the sheep. They must be moved, or where will people park tomorrow?'

Ben moves closer to his mother and gives her a quick hug, while sneaking some cake mix from the bowl. His mother swats him away.

'Pesky boy! Out of that and get going.'

Her loving smile belies the severity of her words.

'It's OK ma. I'll move them straight away, and it'll only take a minute. As soon as they see a bit of hay in the back of the ute, they'll follow me anywhere. And that paddock will be fine to park the visitors' cars in tomorrow, now it's all closely cropped. A bit of sheep manure underfoot will just add to the city slicker's authentic country experience!'

And with a grin and a wave Ben exits from a door near the sink and out into the side garden, whistling for his dog as he goes.

It is clear Ria is expected to help. In a way, this is welcome. In her befuddled state she is not sure that she is capable of doing anything, other than following orders. She moves to the side of the young girl, picks up an apron that is lying nearby on a stool and wraps the ties around her waist. A stylish apron – not – advertising some long forgotten fete and rather grubby at that – but it will do.

The girl looks at her shyly and in a soft Irish accent says:

'Hi, I'm Shelley. Welcome. It's grand you're here in time to give us a hand tomorrow. There's so much to be done.'

Her smile lights up her round face and the slightly anxious look recedes – for a moment. Ria can sense that this girl is feeling uneasy about her arrival but cannot understand why. With the next sentence comes clarity.

'You and I will be sharing the cottage just down the way. I hope you don't mind?'

Ria quickly assures Shelley that this will be fine and sets herself to the task of putting this young girl at ease. As she assists with icing the biscuits together, Ria also focuses on drawing this dainty girl into conversation. All too soon Shelley is in full flow. From time to time Ria's aunt interjects to add further detail. Before long they are all chattering away as if they have known each other for ages. Ria starts to relax, feeling some of the sense of unreality start to drain away. She could be anywhere catching up with friends. Except, she has never before been in such grand surroundings and she knows nothing at all about these people.

She quickly learns that Shelley is 19 and from Dublin. Having finished school last year and now taking a gap year, she has been working with Ria's aunt for some three months. Shelley says she hopes to stay for a while longer, by which time she will have saved enough money to continue with her travels. In a soft aside to Ria, Shelley confesses that she had initially been apprehensive living so far out of town, but her fears had been groundless. She has been having 'so much fun' and would find it hard to move on when her time was up.

Ria's aunt, overhearing the last few words now interjects – no problem with her hearing then – and says she will be sorry to see Shelley go, as she has been 'invaluable with the business.'

'You know: *the business*,' her aunt confides using her hands to signify quotation marks, 'well, it's growing rapidly, and I really need someone to help me to keep up with demand. Of course, it helps that we are so close to Canberra, being our nation's capital and all that, and with so many people living there. It also helps that we have hosted a few celebrity weddings. That publicity is invaluable. Even when they are held in a so-called *secret location*,' again emphasised with now cake-sticky hands, 'the word gets out and we get even more bookings!'

Pouring the cake mix into several large tins and placing them into an electric oven, that is lurking in the shadow of its more impressive Aga cousin, her aunt stretches and says:

'There, that's done. Now we can relax.' Turning and smiling at Ria she continues, 'Welcome my dear. It was such a surprise to hear from you. I was sorry things were so estranged with my sister, but let's not go into that. However, I'm sorry I wasn't there for you or for your mum in recent times. Time for a drink – tea, coffee, wine or water? What'll it be?'

'Anything Aunt Katherina. Perhaps the same as you?'

'None of that Aunt Katherina. I insist you call me Kat, like everyone else does or Aunt Kat if you must. I can't bear my full name. I blame dad you know. He loved Shakespeare and thought he could share that love by calling us those names – Bianca and Katherina. At least we were from the same play!'

'Then you must call me Ria. It seems like mum continued the tradition. Although she seemed to make her selection from the classics, rather than Shakespeare!'

'Ria it is then.'

Holding up a bottle of white wine, which she has just taken out of the refrigerator, Kat asks: 'Will this do?'

'It will be perfect.'

Sometime later, they are all seated around the table and sipping what is described on the bottle's label as a dry local Riesling. The now iced biscuits are packed away in several containers and stacked at the other end of the table.

To Ria's curious questioning her aunt outlines the arrangements for the next day.

'It's fairly straightforward really. The open garden is an annual event which raises funds for local charities. A bit of a pain – and certainly Ben would tell you that. But it's also an excellent opportunity for me to promote this place as a venue. We get good coverage in the media and people come from far and wide. So, tomorrow I already have appointments booked to show interested parties around. Actually, I'm pretty much booked out tomorrow, but there are a few spare time slots later in the day. I suppose it is possible I may get some no shows. And this is where you, Ria, will be helpful. If you don't mind, I'll set you up at a table near the front gate where our visitors will enter the garden, and next to where the open garden folk are collecting the admission payments. You'll be able to greet those who have made an appointment to see me, tick them off my list and tell them what to do. Best if they meet me there at the allotted time. I'll leave some brochures on the table for any others who might be interested. If they want to speak to me you can book them into any of the spare time slots. Twenty minutes is all they will have – but that should be enough.'

Noticing Ria's doubtful expression, her aunt continues 'Don't worry. It's all very simple to manage. I'll run you through our spiel after dinner. It's much more interesting to do so after a few wines!'

Her aunt twinkles at her.

'So, like your mother you are. But I suppose you know that already? The colour of your hair is slightly lighter perhaps? But still with the same range of reddish and gold tones. Hers I think had a fair bit of copper, which I can't see in yours. But as I remember it your eyes are very similar to your mothers. Bluey green like a mountain range – more blue tonight than green but that could be because of your blue top? I suppose they change hue depending on what you wear? And I can see you have the curse of our family's fair skin. Not much use in this climate.'

Getting up she starts fussing over at the Aga.

'Now as soon as that no-good son of mine returns we can eat. It's fairly basic tonight I'm afraid. As a welcoming dinner goes it's pretty average, but it will just have to do. I'm sure you're tired and we will have to be up early tomorrow. The garden club people will be here first thing to set up chairs and stuff. And there will also be food and drink vans to sort out. That part of the organisation is Ben's responsibility.'

Later that evening and still seated around one end of the table, a by now much relaxed Ria starts to feel like she has been part of this household for longer than just a few hours. A freshly washed Ben, attired in clean, but consistently shabby clothes, has joined them. The dinner – roast lamb – *their* lamb Ria is told – not something she feels she really needs to know – with home-made gravy and roast vegetables from the garden. The conversation flows – as does the wine. They have now moved on from the white wine to a local red wine, which Ria finds even more enjoyable. She is not sure how much of the conversation she will remember in the morning given her current state of befuddlement, but she appreciates the general atmosphere of ease and camaraderie that wafts around her. For the most part, she is content to relax and listen to the discussion that is largely focussed on the arrangements for the next day.

By now Ria understands that her help is necessary as all have their designated roles: Aunt Kat with the prospective customers, Ben organising the food and drink vendors and being general go-to person and Shelley preparing the refreshments for the prospective customers.

'We like to give them a sampling of our hospitality to make their initial experience of *Kings View* a welcoming one,' her aunt explains. 'Shelley will be responsible for the refreshments. We will have a sample of an afternoon tea for them to enjoy: the melting moments you just helped to ice, a flourless chocolate cake and some mini – meringues with strawberries and cream. Is that enough do you think? Or should we have some scones as well?'

'Definitely scones,' says Ben. 'After all I have dibbs on the leftovers, so it should be my call.'

Ria can't help but laugh at this. Watching Ben interact with his mother it is clear they are close. The closeness they share is revealed in the way they laugh and gently tease each other. Memories of similar occasions with her mother come flooding back. Waves of grief wash over her as she remembers what she has now lost. She glances down, so no-one can see the tears flooding into her eyes, staring with blurred focus, at hands clasped tightly in her lap. But it has not gone unnoticed. Ben, with a sensitivity she had not expected, speaks up.

'Ma, I think it is time for bed, especially for Cousin Ria here. She's had a big day and we have yet to show her to her bed. Come on cuz,' he says, rising from his chair.

Her aunt also stands, crosses to the pantry and returns with a torch.

'This is for you Ria. Shelley already has her own torch. Just a warning. Do not be tempted to walk to the cottage without the torch, no matter how full the moon. I don't want to scare you, but there are a few things out there that you, as a city dweller, may not expect. A bit like me going to the big city! There I'd certainly would be out of my depth and be desperate for your guidance. So, please pay attention to what I have to share with you.'

Taking Ria's arm, she leads her out into the corridor, through a door and down some steps into the courtyard closely followed by Shelley and Ben. Torches turned on, they shine their way ahead across the paved courtyard, towards a gravel path that leads into the darkening night.

'Always use the torch. I know I've already said that, but there is a reason I am repeating myself. We have dogs and cats and they do their bit to keep the snakes away. But I'm afraid they still like to visit from time to time. Especially in late spring when they're looking for a mate or like now, in early autumn when they're thirsty. Luckily it has been a mild summer, so there's less need for them to look for water. But we still see a few —mostly down by where we keep the hens. I really don't mind that, as they are keeping the mice under control. And sometimes you'll see the odd snake by the pool – cool and damp you know and there could also be frogs to eat.'

As if sensing Ria's unease, she smiles.

'But don't you worry. Just be sensible and pay attention to where you walk. Remember they would rather not see you either!' She adds, 'And a torch helps you avoid those unpleasant mementos that lurk in the shadows – little gifts left by our dogs, like young Fluffy here.' Kat laughs, as she pats the small white dog, now held firmly in her arms. Her laughter lingers as if this is a joke.

Really not funny, Ria thinks to herself, but says nothing.

At the end of the courtyard and past the overhanging tree they crunch along a gravel path that bisects what she thinks must be a rose garden judging from the heavy fragrance wafting in the night air, and then they all stop at a wooden gate in a low stone wall.

'This is where I'll leave you girls. Goodnight to you both. If you can be up at the house by 7.30 in the morning that should give us sufficient time to get organised. Please wear decent clothes – and that goes for you too Ben!'

Aunt Kat opens the gate and waves Shelley and Ria through. The fluffy white dog gently deposited on the ground and taking Ben's arm in hers, Kat turns and fades into the darkness heading back to the old house, now a black shadow outlined against the deepening sky.

'This way,' murmurs Shelley, shining her torch onto the gravel track that leads to another looming shadow nearby. Through another gate, smaller this time, they enter a fenced off yard and then, climbing up two stairs onto a porch, they approach the front door.

'It's really tiny – only two bedrooms and an enclosed veranda out the back, but it's cosy. See, in here,' she says, turning on a light and then pointing to the first doorway to the right opening off a small sitting room. 'This is your bedroom. I'm in the room next door. Through here another sitting room with an open fire, which can really pump out the heat. The kitchen's really small, but you'll find we don't use it much. And down that hallway to the back veranda you will find the bathroom and toilet – again tiny, but as we spend most of our time up at the big house, it doesn't really matter what our accommodation is like.'

Ria quickly glances into her new sleeping quarters and likes what she sees. It is simple but looks like it will be comfortable. Polished wooden floors, a double bed freshly made up with crisp white linen, a fluffy blue and white striped doona and draped at the foot of the bed a soft blanket in a pale shade of blue. A multi-drawer pine dressing table topped with an oval mirror is set against the wall opposite the bed. In the corner, a matching wardrobe and under the window a padded window seat. Perfect for sitting and relaxing she thinks - although she is fast coming to understand that there may be little time for that!

In the corner, she can see her bags have been left – by Ben, she assumes. He must have brought them here before dinner, whilst he was out and about doing his chores.

She hears Shelley call and wanders out to find her. Through a doorway into a sitting room, then down a corridor and out onto a small, enclosed veranda and into a tiny bathroom.

'See I told you it was small. But it all works. You'll have to shower in the bathtub, but at least the water is always hot. I'm off to bed now. In the morning, you'll see the view. It's rather pretty. We look out across to a wee brook out the back. When it rains and the brook runs fast we can hear the water rush by. But for now, it's rather quiet. Norma, our neighbour, lives next door in a dolls house cottage like ours. She makes no noise. In fact, I very rarely see her. She's old I think.'

She gives Ria a quick tap on the arm as she pushes past.

'If you're not up by 7, I will wake you. Good night now. Sweet dreams.'

As Ria moves around her bedroom, quickly unpacking her bags and hanging what needs to be hung in the wardrobe, she ponders the adventure that has been today and considers the confusion she now feels.

If anyone had told her six months ago that she would be visiting a grand country estate owned by people that she was told were her relatives, she would have scoffed and accused them of hallucinating. Yet, here she was, with people who were family, yet no more known to her than strangers in the street. These relatives whose life was so different to hers, taking for granted all the space and luxury that surrounded them and comfortable with the company of venomous creatures and disgusting farmyard aromas. As a city girl for all her life Ria feels puzzled as to how such things could be accepted with apparent calm. Even now, when opening her bedroom window and breathing in the evening air redolent with the aroma of cow manure and possibly sheep manure, she wonders how she will ever become accustomed to such disgusting odours.

The absence of sound is another thing. Growing up in Sydney, and especially in Glebe which had been the only home she has ever known, there had always been the distant hum from the chaos of city traffic, punctuated by the siren call of ambulances or fire engines. Surrounded too by the ever-present sounds from people living their lives around her – laughing, calling, yelling, and sometimes screaming. Always something. Now – there was no sound at all – no wait – just then a rustle outside, then followed by a bark. A soft bark, a reminder of what she would hear when watching those English countryside television shows set in picturesque rural settings. Could it be a fox? She shines her torch out the window into the darkness. Two small golden orbs of light are reflected back at her. Then those lights vanish, and she hears the sound of something stealthily moving away through the vegetation. Supressing a shudder, she quickly closes the window and turns away heading back towards her half-unpacked bags.

It is not until sometime later when she is lying in her bed that thoughts of home and loved ones resurface. Flooding into her mind are thoughts of her mother, who for so long had been a constant point of reference in her life. Now she feels adrift, no anchor to hold her secure or in one place. But would she find echoes of her mother here? Surely this place must once have been familiar to her mother. After all, by her calculations, Aunt Kat being the elder sibling had been married and a mother before Bianca ran away from home. Surely, she must have been here at times, sat in that kitchen, ate at that enormous table and walked in the courtyard. Maybe discovering those stories of her mother's early life will bring her some comfort? But for now she is not so sure.

As waves of exhaustion battle with feelings of sorrow Ria struggles to latch onto any positive thought to keep her afloat. The image of Ben striding towards her, arms held out wide plays out in her mind's eye. That smile, those sunny eyes – that scruffy appearance in need of a make-over. Perhaps spending time getting to know her cousin will bring its own rewards? At least after another day spent in this strange environment things may become more familiar, and perhaps she might start to feel like she has a place in this family. With a sigh, she turns over, snuggles into the doona, and surrenders to unconsciousness.

Chapter Four

Next morning, as she struggles to awareness, Ria's first thought is that a torch is shining in her face. But then she realises it is sunlight pouring through the bedroom window.

Must remember to draw the curtains tonight she reminds herself as she reaches for her watch to check the time. It is early. Plenty of time for a shower before she must present herself at the big house.

No absence of sound this morning. Nearby she can hear the rooster proclaiming the successful arrival of another day. In the distance, the cacophony brought about by a regular barking of dogs. The rhythmic chugging of a tractor engine, evidence that someone else is already up and about, and at work.

Apart from the challenges of climbing into a deep bathtub, the shower experience passes uneventfully. The water is hot and plentiful and does much to revive her for the day ahead. Once dressed in what she hopes is acceptable attire, Ria boils the kettle and with mug of tea in hand, wanders out the back door to investigate her surroundings.

The cottage, as Shelley indicated last night, is built on a rise above the small creek they passed over yesterday when she and Ben approached the farm. On the other side of the flowing water black cows and calves graze on a dewy creek flat. On this side there is clearly a paddock surrounding the cottage. But for now, this paddock is empty of livestock.

The henhouse or chook-yard to use the common expression, must be nearby she thinks, judging from the level of noise – of crowing and clucking. But not too nearby Ria hopes, feeling apprehensive about a possible snake encounter.

Two other almost identical cottages are visible, also along the creek, but not too close. The only sign of life from these cottages is a wispy ribbon of smoke drifting from one chimney. Recalling Shelley's words from the night before, she wonders if smoking chimney indicates residence by the mysterious, seldom seen Norma.

Wandering slowly around the yard, Ria takes her time to inspect the garden and review her surroundings. Sipping her tea as she progresses, she struggles to identify the various plants. Her mother had always been the gardener in her family and despite her mother's persistent attempts, Ria's knowledge of plants is limited. She can see that it is a simple garden. Roses line the path up to the front door with a few daisies in the flower bed by the porch. Some small trees are scattered, seemingly at random around the yard, all rather charming, but lacking the grandeur of the extensive garden up at the big house. Stepping up onto the front porch she makes herself comfortable in an ancient, padded cane chair and waits …and thinks.

Ria is still unsure why she should be here. What made her latch onto the invitation to come and stay and, why visit immediately the invitation was offered? She already has a home and a job in Sydney. No, not just a job. A career. Why then, she wonders, did her mother consider it so important to leave that letter, urging her to return to this part of the world? After all her mother had left here long ago, never to return or even mention that this place and the people in it existed. What did her mother hope for her to gain? Sure, her aunt and cousin seem lovely, but at this stage of her adult life, did she need to know them? Given they had been absent from her life up until now, then not knowing them would be no loss? And where was the uncle? She realises no-one had mentioned him last night and there was no reference to him in her mother's letter. Was this an ominous sign?

How long should she stay here? Last night it was clear that her aunt was not contemplating a rushed visit. But Ria has never been a free-loader and she feels reluctant to take advantage of this family, despite their warm welcome. At least for today she knows she is needed, so maybe it is just a matter of letting things flow and taking it one day at a time? With the trauma and emotion of recent times this thought gives her some comfort. She stands and goes inside to wash her mug and wake Shelley who, despite her assurances last night of waking up early, is still asleep.

Walking up to the big house in the bright light of morning, Ria is overwhelmed by the size of the garden that surrounds her. Shelley keeps up a constant discourse on the points of interest, almost as if she is an experienced tour guide, which may be exactly what she is as part of her day job. The beauties of the rose garden are pointed out to Ria, the convict built shed and stables visible some distance away are observed, and the various stone walls that define the yard, partially obscured by climbing roses, are also admired.

They cross the courtyard and enter the kitchen where they find Ria's aunt in a flap.

'Quick girls. Grab some toast and then we need to get sorted. Ben's outside showing the stall owners where to set up. The plan is to place them over near the tennis court. I think Ben has already set out chairs and tables on the tennis court, so that's one thing done at least.'

She takes a breath and smiles, 'Thank goodness it's a beautiful day. Good weather always brings out the crowds.'

With that, all three turn towards the window to observe the day unfolding before them. It is a perfect autumn day. Clear skies, dew still on the ground, the temperature cool, but with the promise of warmth as the day progresses.

Aunt Kat surveys with pride that patch of the garden apparent from the kitchen window.

'We couldn't have picked a better time to show off the garden. The last flush of roses, the nerines in all their glory and the trees, just on the turn. I know some might prefer spring, with all that blossom and leaf bud. But then we would have been plagued with hay fever and spring showers. All that boggy ground and handing out of tissues and umbrellas. No thanks! That's so not for me!'

With a glance at Shelley and Ria she once again focuses on the job at hand. Clearly her aunt is someone used to being in command. Now Aunt Kat is in full flood, issuing a stream of instructions at Shelley. Shelley, Ria can see, is experienced in Aunt Kat's style. An attentive look on her face as she listens intently and then, following each command received, she merely nods and smiles. Shelley is expected to be in charge of the refreshments for the people meeting Aunt Kat and is dispatched to set up trays in readiness.

'I'll bring our visitors into the formal lounge for refreshments while I explain the venue options. After that I'll answer any questions and then give them a brief tour around to show them the garden and what facilities are available. Here, Shelley this is your copy of the timetable. If you can make sure a tray is ready for each visitor and the tea and coffee are ready to be made as soon as each lot of guests arrive that will be fine. Now for you Ria. I'll take you down to your post by the front gate. Here, take this water bottle with you, as you'll be there for some time. Oh, and carry these please.'

A box of leaflets is thrust into her hands along with a full bottle of water and Ria then stumbles after her aunt, who, similarly laden, bustles out the door, seemingly unhandicapped by her load.

By the gate into the garden two stalls have already been erected. Numerous people of a not so certain age bustle with purpose, draping cloths over folding tables, erecting signs, conferring, and generally making themselves busy with every appearance of people with something important to do.

Aunt Kat's arrival is welcomed as if she is a person of note. A number of people call out greetings, while others take their turn to share with Aunt Kat items of what they consider to be essential information. With the skill of a diplomat Aunt Kat listens, calmly issues decrees, and then moves onto the next issue. Ria, standing nearby is mute with admiration. Then Aunt Kat remembers her existence and calls her over.

'Everyone. Now listen up. Let me introduce you all to my niece Ria, who will be in charge of my stall here today. If anyone comes to you today with questions about venue hire, please direct them to Ria. She'll be able to help them and answer any queries.'

Ria is conscious of the many faces regarding her with curiosity and, by and large, welcoming smiles on their faces. She tries to muster up a smile in response and gives a little wave with her not so free hand.

'Here, Ria, just pop that box of leaflets behind this table. Then help me with these banners please.'

The two banners proclaiming *Kings View Venue Hire – Historic venue for weddings, parties and celebrations* are smoothed out. One banner affixed on the front of the now draped table and the other attached to the back wall of the plastic sheeted shelter in which the table is located.

'That will just have to do. It's not too bad I suppose,' says Aunt Kat, standing back and observing their work.

'Now please fan those pamphlets out on the table. We still need a bit of colour though. I'll just run and get some flowers. That should do it – oh - and spread out these business cards too.'

She quickly returns with a squat vase of freshly cut roses and a name tag for Ria to wear. Under the heading *Kings View*, Ria can see her name has been scrawled in marker pen.

'Here, pin this on you and take this timetable. When people inquire about their appointment, please ask them to make sure they are here at the table at the correct time, and I will come and meet them. If they don't turn up, then we can at least try them on their mobile phone, that is if they have one. You'll see their contact numbers on the timetable. I must leave you now. Other things to do you know – but please read the brochure. It has all the information you will need to become an expert on *Kings View* and answer any questions. And don't forget there are still some spare times available at the end of the day, in case someone wants to make an appointment. Here's a pen. Are you OK?'

Ria feels as if she has no choice but to nod. Especially as she sees her aunt's frazzled expression clear at her nod.

'Good girl. What a life saver you are!'

And with that her aunt is off trotting across the lawn back to the house and leaving Ria in charge of her little stall. All around her, scenes of activity – voices raised in inquiry and response, sounds of hammering, beeping of reversing vehicles and people scurrying to and fro in attitudes of great importance.

She settles herself down on the folding canvas chair beside the table, picks up a brochure and starts to read.

A short while later Ria feels she knows all about *Kings View*. *An historic residence a short distance from the village of Kings Vale and a scenic drive from Canberra* is what she reads. The brochure, full of images of the gracious house and rambling gardens have convinced her, that if she was looking for a venue, then this would be the place for her. After all, she thinks: *who would not want to pretend that all of this was theirs for a day?*

The stall has been placed immediately next to the admissions tent which has been erected beside the only available access gate into the garden. Although it is not yet officially opening time, some eager visitors are already arriving, paying their admission fees and wandering across to her stall, where they immediately pick up and start to read the brochure.

Ria pastes what she hopes is a welcoming smile on her face and greets these early visitors. She hopes all day won't be like this or her face will soon have a fake smile frozen in place. She welcomes the visitors and quickly discovers that each interaction is different. Some are locals and regular visitors to the garden. They are only interested in finding out the location of her aunt – in the house – that's easy. Others want to know the location of the plant stall – as if she knows – but a nearby official overhears the question and steps in to assist. Another wants to know the location of the toilets – well, even that is obvious to Ria – and she points to the line of Porta Loos out by the front gate.

It is soon 10am, time for the first appointment. Ria looks around for the potential customers who have arranged to meet her aunt. No sign of them. But then again, there is no sign of her aunt. She looks around anxiously. There is little she can do but wait. To her relief she sees a young couple walking briskly towards her with purpose. Hand in hand they reach her and stare at Ria.

'Hello. Is this where we meet Mrs Kingsley for our appointment?' the young man asks.

Ria can sense waves of anxiety emanating from them and points to two seats by the table.

'Yes, it is. Just take a seat. It shouldn't be too long. Let me cross you off our list. You must be Jonathan Richards and Helena Morrison?'

They nod and turn eager eyes toward her. Ria feels like she is now in the company of two nervy children. Never before has she felt much older than her 25 years, but in the presence of these two she now feels positively ancient. In an effort to calm them she makes small talk and soon learns they are getting married and want to hold their reception at *Kings View*.

'We both live in the village,' the young girl says in a childlike confiding tone.

Glancing at her partner, who has enfolded her hand in his, she continues: 'You see, my grandma lived here once - when it was grander and there was lots of help. She worked in the house and my grandpa worked on the farm. So, when we decided to get married we thought it would be nice for us all to be here where it once was home. It feels somehow right.'

Her voice trails off and she looks hesitantly at Ria, almost as if she is seeking Ria's approval. Ria feels a need to reassure this child bride so she launches into what she hopes is the appropriate response, but sounds to her ears like meaningless babble. With a profound sense of relief, she sees her aunt approaching at speed.

'Ah, here's my aunt now. She'll show you around and answer all your questions. Take this brochure with you – and good luck with the wedding.'

The young couple smile shyly in response as Ria hands them over to her aunt. Crossing their names off the list she wonders if all the potential customers will be as sweet as those two.

Of course, they are not. By mid-afternoon she is amazed at the variety of people considering the house and garden as a venue for their celebration. By and large the intended event will be a wedding, but occasionally she is told that people are considering the venue for a christening or birthday celebration. Even a surprise wedding anniversary event for some lucky parents.

'But how to get them here so it will be a surprise,' a weathered farming type confides in her. 'It's their golden wedding anniversary and I want it to be special for them. They both love the garden here, so I thought they might enjoy an afternoon tea in the courtyard with friends and family. But I want it to be a surprise.'

'Your parents are friendly with my aunt?' Ria asks, thinking quickly.

He nods.

'Well, I'm sure we could think of something. What about if you say you are taking them for a drive and just drop in to say hello? Or.' She glances at his weathered face and hands: 'could there be a reason for you to visit – say to look at stock that's for sale or lend a hand and maybe suggest they come and keep you company and possibly say hello to my aunt, if she is at home. Would they believe that?'

His face clears.

'Yes, that would work. My dad always likes checking out another farmer's stock and my mum never turns down a chance for a chat. Well done young lady. You are a gem!'

Others are not so easy to manage. A mother of the bride with a voice that screeched with false refinement was more of a challenge. As this woman made it more than clear that she considered Ria her inferior, Ria found herself hoping that her aunt would be doubling the hiring fee for this one. She suspects that whatever they did would not be good enough for this woman.

A professional couple dressed in designer clothes, provide Ria with some entertainment. The man, a bit of a dish she thinks, like some of the surgeons at her hospital, carries a notepad on which she can see a long list of dot points. Presumably questions for her aunt.

How pleased her aunt will be, she thinks, *or most likely – not!*

The dishy man ushers his glossy and glam partner to a chair, and then proceeds to grill Ria.

Maybe not a surgeon, maybe a barrister, she thinks.

'Where is Mrs Kingsley? Will this take long? We are very busy you know and cannot wait.'

Nope, definitely a surgeon, she decides. *So important and so busy. Unlike us mere mortals, they cannot wait.*

Luckily Ria is experienced in dealing with types like this.

'Do please take a seat. I'm sure you won't be kept waiting long. So many people want to hire this venue and my aunt has back-to-back appointments all day and you know…' at this Ria grimaces and raises her eyebrows, 'sometimes people forget the time and go over a few minutes as they have so many questions.' This said with a glimpse at his long list of questions.

Ria continues, before he can take offence:

'But she has prepared some home cooked treats for you to have with tea and coffee. I'm sure after the long drive here you will be needing some refreshments, and you'll be able to relax in the formal sitting room while you chat with my aunt'.

Seeing them eye off the brochures, Ria adds:

'Do you have a brochure? …. No? Well please take one … or two.'

The bride-to-be takes a handful of the brochures. Ria wonders not so charitably if they need a few extra to assist with boasting rights with their friends.

Trying to sound genuinely interested, which Ria isn't, Ria then asks about the proposed function.

'Are you interested in hiring this venue for a wedding or for something else?'

And with that they are off. Tumbling over each other in their eagerness to show off and share their story, all details are soon divulged to Ria. Renewing their vows in front of friends, children and family. Ten years on, and people said it would never last. Second marriages for both of them, the woman confides. The man discloses that he saw an article concerning a celebrity who renewed her vows at an historic mansion, with her children as attendants. How, after reading that article he decided that if it was good enough for her, then it would work for them. Under the blustery confidence in his speech Ria could detect a hint of defiance – a this will show them attitude and for a moment her opinion of these two softens.

The day has progressively become warmer. With each hour, more people arrive – family groups, garden tour groups, bus tours, loving couples and children – so many children. Running along the winding garden paths, chasing each other across the lawns. Laughing, crying or yelling – but never silent.

Some distance away she can see a gardening expert talking to a mass of people wearing sensible shoes, sensible hats and of course, sensible clothes. So far away that Ria cannot hear a word the expert is saying – and for that she is grateful.

Wandering past, another person leading a group, pausing now and then to pontificate on some feature of the house or garden. For a moment, when they draw near, she can hear a snippet of his commentary.

'From here you can see the front of the residence. The two-storey entrance and to the left – the single level two roomed extension. I say two roomed, but they are not small rooms. One is the formal sitting room which looks in both directions through windows still with the original glass – out to the front and in the other direction onto the courtyard. Off the sitting room another room, which was originally the ballroom and was used regularly by friends and neighbours in times past. They had to make their own fun you know, living in such an isolated place. This part of the building was built in the late Nineteenth Century from stone quarried on the property, with the local red brick used as facing around the windows and on the corners of the building.'

He pauses, listens to a question from someone in the group, and then continues: 'the original house? Oh, yes, probably built around 1830, when the family arrived here. Pre-Queen Victoria which I suppose is why it's called *Kings View* and not *Queens View* and the same applies for the village. Although I quite like the sound of *Queens Vale* for the village. Hah!' he chuckles and then continues, 'Now, where was I? The original house? Well, it has largely been subsumed by this rather grand residence, but a few key points are still visible around the back. If you follow me this way, I'll point them out to you...'

With that the group moves on, tamely following their leader, like so many ducklings behind a mother duck.

For a moment Ria is disappointed. She has learnt more in two minutes, from a complete stranger, than she has learnt from her family. But then again, she reminds herself, she did only arrive yesterday. Since then there has been a turmoil of activity and no time for any background briefings. A little voice in her head whispers in complaint. If her mother had been honest with her daughter and told her all, then there would not be this black hole in her past. How could her mother do this to her? What could have been so bad or gone so wrong that her mother felt the need to completely wipe out all that had come before?

A torrent of emotion threatens to overwhelm her, as these feelings of loss and rage swirl around in Ria's head. Just in time a cup, well a disposable cup, of coffee is placed on the table before her. She looks up into the laughing sapphire eyes of her newfound cousin.

'Here, have this. You look like you need it. It's coffee – so they say. But I make no promises. It could be something worse,' Ben grins at her, his eyes twinkling and his smile revealing surprisingly white and even teeth.

His attire may have started the day as clean rural cool, but somehow his inner Ben has triumphed. The shirt tails hang free, the moleskin trousers which she recalls were spotless earlier this morning, display green stains on the knees and grubby marks on the sides, which she assumes are a result of frequent hand wiping. Now removing his Akubra hat Ria can see that his hair – well, it is just like yesterday – still threatening to escape.

Staring at his hair with wonder, Ria asks: 'have you ever thought about a haircut?'

Blue eyes crinkle with amusement.

'Are you channelling my mother? I say no to haircuts! This is my artistic genius breaking through. Country life may try to constrain me, but my inner artist will always triumph.'

He ends this with a flourish throwing his arms out wide and sloshing some of his coffee onto the grass.

'Bugger. Well never mind. It's pretty awful stuff, as you will soon discover.'

Ria pays those words no attention as she is still processing his earlier statement.

'An artist. You?'

'Yes ma'am. You may be surprised to learn that I'm a man of hidden depths! Not just easy on the eye you know! Once upon a time I went to arts school and studied to be a sculptor. I still do a bit - when sheep aren't lambing, cows aren't calving, horses aren't foaling, fences don't need fixing and so on and so on.' Ben grimaces as he says this, and then continues: 'so, as you might suspect I don't get much spare time to do anything artistic. But I can show you my latest if you want? Once all this circus is finished that is – maybe tomorrow, when it's a bit quieter?'

'Yes please. I would so like to see that. And just to learn more about you and your family. I know so little.'

With that Ben's face clouds over. The smile fades and the happiness that was shining through now disappears, subsumed by a sombre expression.

'Well, maybe it's not worth knowing. It's possible that once you learn more about us you may want to run far away and forget all about this family. You said your mother didn't tell you anything about us. That could be for a reason. Have you thought about that?'

The arrival of the next appointment – another love-struck couple puts an end to the conversation. With a wave of his hand Ben turns and disappears into the crowd, but not before he promises to return later on. Ria watches him go and soon sees him deep in conversation with another, similarly attired young man. As she watches, they turn and Ria can see Ben pointing her out to his companion.

Now what can they be talking about? she wonders. From what she can see at this distance, Ben's companion looks like someone worth further investigating. With his broad shoulders and athletic build, she hopes she might get to meet him. They both notice her looking at them, laugh, wave in her direction and then turn away, wandering off still engrossed in their discussion.

By late afternoon Ria decides she is a natural. She can now recite a great patter to all interested parties, sound genuinely concerned about people's inquiries and has become practised in soothing those waiting for her aunt, who gets later and later for each subsequent appointment. Each time she finally appears, her aunt looks increasingly exhausted. When Ria asks if there is anything further she can do to help, her aunt brushes her off.

'No dear. You and Shelley are doing wonders as it is. I don't know how I would have managed without you here.' Her aunt runs her hand through her hair and continues: 'but no more new appointments. Just take their phone numbers and tell them I'll ring them in the next day or so, to arrange a time for a *private viewing*' – using her hands as quotation marks. 'Maybe that'll appease them.'

Ria deals with all further inquiries with ease and speaking with more authority than she knew she possessed. Maybe it helped, but after she explained that the owner was her aunt, people seemed to accept whatever she told them. If only they knew, she thought, that less than twenty-four hours into this new life, she knew as little as they did about the Kingsley's and their concerns.

The open garden was meant to end by 4.30 in the afternoon. Yet by 5pm people were still milling around, sitting in groups under the trees and generally enjoying themselves. The food vendors were experiencing a last-minute rush to their vans, especially the ice cream van, in front of which a queue of fidgeting children and anxious parents grew as she watched.

The attendants at the adjoining table assured her in cheery tones that their takings were well beyond their expectations. Now focussing on packing up, they bid her farewell and left Ria sitting alone at her table, uncertain as to whether she should also pack up and leave. The last of the appointments were now with her aunt, and no more were expected. But what if a potential customer came by? Ria feels that she owes it to her aunt to linger. Ben, however, clearly has other ideas. Sneaking up from behind her, the first she knew of his presence was the pressure of his hands on her shoulders. With a squeal of fright Ria jumped up and turned to glare at her laughing cousin.

'Come on coz. Day is done. You've earned a drink. Come and meet some of my friends.'

He takes her by the hand and leads her over to a group of people sitting on the grass under an enormous elm tree.

'Hey everyone. This here is my cousin Ria. She's visiting from Sydney, but don't you hold it against her! Ria, I won't tell you all their names, as there are far too many for you to remember. Here, have a drink,' he says, as he thrusts a bottle of beer into her hands.

In response to a chorus of 'hello Ria', 'hi' and 'how ya', Ria waves and then sits down. Beer is not her usual drink of choice, but after the long hot day the first sip tastes like nectar. She takes another sip, then looks cautiously around at the crowd of people who have now resumed their conversations. All of them appear to be about Ben's age – late 20's she estimates, although some of the women could be younger. And mostly country people, judging from their attire, which is a sort of consistent uniform of faded jeans or moleskins, checked shirts and riding boots. Ria looking down at her outfit of black jeans, black t-shirt, chains looped around her neck and Doc Martens on her feet and realises she stands out like the city girl that she is.

The man at the other side of Ben leans forwards and holds out his hand for her to shake. It is the man she saw earlier talking to Ben. Tall and muscled. Strong forearms revealed by pushed up shirt sleeves. Short crinkle-curled dark hair, a face dominated by determined jawline and amber eyes that smile a welcome.

What's not to like?

'Hi. I'm Gordon but call me Geordie. Everyone else does. Welcome to this part of the world and to us. I hope you're staying for a while?' he says, looking hopeful.

Ben elbows him.

'Only if you're nice to her. All of you. On your best behaviour now. I don't want to scare off my only cousin!'

To calls from the others – 'as if', 'it's you that will scare her off you wally' and so on, Ria finds herself laughing and relaxing into the moment. Feeling comfortable like she has ended up with a group of old friends, Ria joins in the conversation as if she has known them all for ages. And they treat her the same way. Before long Ria learns that Geordie has been Ben's best friend since kindergarten and lives on a neighbouring farm. Some of the others live on nearby farms, some in the village and others who are old school or university friends have driven out from Canberra for the day. They are obviously all known to each other and judging from the conversation that flows, it soon becomes clear to Ria that some are couples.

By evening the farm once again settles back into its usual quiet serenity, only punctuated by the calls of stock and birdlife. It is as if the confusion and noise of the day had never occurred. The flattened grass, and the line of Porta Loos awaiting collection, are all that remains of the chaos, the only evidence of the hordes that had descended on the garden. The farm dogs finally released from their forced confinement in the kennels, happily roam around the garden ferreting out scraps of discarded food, tracking interesting scents and once more delighting in their freedom.

Aunt Kat, Ben, Shelley and Ria sit inside around the kitchen table, picking at what amounts to that evening's meal. Some cheese and crackers followed by fruit and left-over cake is all any of them have the energy to face. Desultory conversation ensues. They sit in companionable silence, occasionally broken by intermittent comments, as different thought bubbles surface in their minds.

'So many gluten intolerant folks,' says Shelley. 'Luckily the cake was made with almond flour, or they would have been very unhappy.'

Aunt Kat nods. 'But it went well. We have a number of confirmed bookings for spring and a few afternoon celebrations inside in winter. Some people like to celebrate by a roaring fire. Birthday celebrations I think and so much easier to organise. No marquees to erect. And Ria's done well. I see I have heaps of inquiries to follow up next week. Thank you dear. Your first day and you were a star! I promise life isn't usually this hectic!'

'Yeah right,' says Ben, as he and Shelley exchange amused glances which belie the truth of Aunt Kat's words.

Ben turns to his mother.

'Ma I was thinking that now Ria's here, why doesn't Shelley have a break? After all she is meant to be having a holiday – with her gap year and all that - and she has yet to get to Sydney.'

Clearly Ben has not rehearsed this with Shelley. Her eyes widen and a big grin appears, and then fades as she contemplates Ria's aunt.

'Only if you can spare me Kat?' she says.

'Of course, I can. We have two weeks until the next function. And I have Ben and Ria to help if anything unexpected happens. Go and make your plans. You deserve a break. Would you like to go to Sydney? It's very easy to get there from here. You could catch the train like Ria did.'

Ria pipes up. 'I'm sure you could stay at my home in Glebe. Not exactly my home – more like Penny's home. But I will call her if you want and arrange things. You could have my bedroom. But don't let her rope you into working for her. She still runs the BnB accommodation that my mum established. Well, runs may not be the right term – manages might be more accurate. We hired someone to run it when mum fell ill and could no longer do much. Penny and I couldn't take it on because of our jobs. Penny's a lecturer at the university and what with my nursing, we had no spare time to help. I don't know what Penny will now do with the business....' Ria's voice trails off and her eyes cloud over as she contemplates the future that includes so many variables that still need to be sorted.

She gives her head a shake as if to dispel those thoughts and continues: 'I'll ring Penny if you want and speak to her about having you to stay. I should ring her anyway to let her know I've arrived safely. You'll love Glebe. So close to the city and the harbour and so full of life – students, trendies and still a few of the original inhabitants. OK with you?'

'Oh, yes please.' Shelley is beside herself with excitement. 'I've been wanting to visit Sydney, but didn't know where to stay, or how to arrange it. Kat would you be able to spare me next week?'

'Of course, child. You deserve a break. Now, if you'll all please excuse me it's time for a good dose of something mindless – not you lot, but something on tv or in a book. I don't mind what it is so long as I don't have to speak or think. I've just had it with being nice to people all day.'

With that Aunt Kat arises, takes her plates to the sink and then leaves the room followed as always, by her faithful fluffy white dog.

'Well, I must go too,' says Ben, standing up and heading for the door, used plates left on the table. 'Dogs to be fed and shut away you know. See you both in the morning.'

He stops, turns back as if struck by a new thought.

'Ria, do you ride?'

'Well, sort of. Nothing fancy though.'

A bit of an overstatement that. Riding lessons in early teens do not an accomplished rider make. But hey, Ria thinks to herself, it must be like riding a bicycle – once learnt never forgotten.

'Excellent. That will be enough. Fancy a ride around the boundaries tomorrow, after breakfast? It'll help you get your bearings?'

Ria nods, not quite sure what such a ride would entail, but how could she refuse?

As they walk back to the cottage, by torchlight of course, Shelley is in full spate chattering with enthusiasm about her impending visit to Sydney.

'Thank you so much for your offer. I know I could've stayed in a hostel, but after being here with your aunt and Ben, that would've felt a bit lonely. Being in Sydney with your not quite aunt or whatever she is, will be so much better. It will still feel like being part of a family and I miss my family so much.' Her voice gives a bit of a wobble, as she snakes out her hand and puts it on Ria's arm as if to emphasise the point.

'It's no problem. I just hope you have fun. The house will be busy with guests coming and going, but that is part of the fun. Whatever you do don't let Penny rope you into doing any of the work. I know how persuasive she can be.'

'Don't you worry. I'm happy to help. If only to pay for my board,' she says in her soft Irish brogue.

'Oh, gosh. If you do then Penny will never let you go, and then we'll all be in terrible trouble with Aunt Kat!'

Laughing at that and at total ease with each other, arm in arm they enter the cottage. Bidding Shelley a good night Ria enters her bedroom and collapses on her bed. A little over 24 hours in this place and she feels like she has been in this strange new world for so much longer. Her Aunt Kat, clearly burdened by the pressures of running a commercial operation seemed on first impressions to be a kind and practical person, albeit with an aura of sadness around her.

Yet the love for her son shines through and her pleasure at meeting her newfound niece appears to be genuine.

Why then, Ria wonders, did her mother break off all contact with her sister and her family? And Ben. What is she to make of him? Funny and kind. Look how he brought her coffee today. And a person with hidden talents – well, possibly. She will leave a final decision on that until after she has inspected his artistic output. He appears to be much liked, judging by the large group of friends that came to share the day with him. Interesting friends who might be worth knowing better – especially his long-time friend – Geordie wasn't it?

Maybe, Ria thinks to herself, maybe this visit isn't going too badly after all. With feelings of contentment jostling with an overwhelming sense of exhaustion, she rolls over, pulls up the quilt and surrenders to unconsciousness.

Chapter Five

Next morning after breakfast Aunt Kat and Shelley shoo Ria out of the kitchen, assuring her they have plenty to do in her absence.

'To be sure you will just get under our feet if you hang about,' says Shelley, giving Ria a quick push. 'Off you go – find some riding boots from the pile out there in the mud room,' she adds, giving her a further push in the direction of the enclosed porch off the kitchen.

'Yes, go Ria,' her aunt reinforces the command. 'Ben is already over at the stables, waiting for you. Go,' this time said with a wave of the hand. 'We have heaps to do here. You won't be missed. Take your time and don't rush back.'

In the enclosed porch Ria discovers two shelves of riding boots and wellington boots of various sizes and condition. A pair selected and put on, Ria opens the door and heads off in the direction indicated. A gravel path leads from the side door past a tennis court that has seen better days, and on towards a small gate. Through this gate Ria enters a paddock, which she crosses and then arrives at a set of yards and some stables. The stables, about six of them, each open on to their own yard with gates at the far end giving access to a large paddock. Horses grazing in that paddock lift their heads and contemplate her approach. As if they realise Ria has no food for them, the horses then drop their heads and resume grazing. In one of the yards Ben is busy saddling a stocky chestnut horse.

'Ah, there you are then. Good morning. Feeling fully recovered from yesterday's excitement?' he asks with a smile.

Ria assures him that she is fit and rested.

'Slept like a lamb,' she tells him.

'So did I! Thank goodness open gardens are an annual event. It would do me in otherwise! But enough of that. Come and meet your new best friend. Ria meet Tonka. Tonka meet Ria. Here, hold out your hand for Tonka to sniff. Yes, like that. He's very friendly. See he likes you already. But don't let him rub on you. When did you last ride?'

Now that the ride is fast becoming a reality Ria worries she has misled Ben and tries to explain to him the limitations of her skills. Ben waves her away.

'Don't stress. You'll be fine. Tonka here is a real gentleman and you'll be in a stock saddle which will hold you in and on. His canter, if you get that far, is a dream. Like sitting in an armchair. And his lope is heaven. He's a quarter horse you see – was my sister's horse. She did everything on him. Pony club, stock work and competing at the local show.'

'Your sister?' Ria tries hard not to sound too surprised. This is the first she has heard of a sister.

'Yeah, my sister Kitty.'

'Where is she?'

Ben's voice slows. Ria can sense that he is reluctant to elaborate.

'Long story. I'll tell you later. Not now. We need to get moving. Let's just say for now that she is gone – long gone. Here,' he says, handing her Tonka's reins, 'Hold him while I get you a riding helmet. I think Kitty's should fit you. Then you can get mounted and walk around a bit, while I get my horse. Fidget is her name. Fidget by name, Fidget by nature. She's waiting in her stable. All saddled and ready to go.'

It is clear to Ria that Ben has no intention of sharing any further information about his sister. She can tell this by the closed expression on his face and his focus on the task at hand. Now is not the time for an exchange of confidences between cousins. Maybe she has yet to earn that right? After all, she reminds herself. Ben barely knows her, so how can she expect him to trust her with disclosures that are so obviously painful to him? Likewise, how can she expect him to understand how frustrating this is for her to be drip-fed information? But it is also not the time to insist on being told. She tells herself she must wait for the opportunity to arise, when a clear invitation is issued to share further information, and then pounce.

Ben goes into what must be the tack shed located towards the end of the row of stables and returns with a riding helmet for Ria. She tries it on and, with some adjustment to the chin strap, it fits. He leads Tonka over to a mounting block, and holds the horse while Ria mounts her steed. Or to be more accurate scrambles on, while steed and Ben wait patiently. Ben fiddles with the girth and the stirrup straps and then stands back considering.

'Yep. That looks good. Let me know if the stirrups don't feel ok, but better a fraction too short than too long. Now just walk him around the yard while I get old Fidget. He's trained for western riding or hacking, so he will neck rein, or you can use the reins normally – whatever you like – or you can just shift your weight in the saddle, and he will understand. Like I said, this old man is perfect.'

Ten years, Ria thinks as she urges Tonka forward. *It must be ten years since I last sat in a saddle on a horse. I may have forgotten a lot about riding, but I have not forgotten how wonderful it feels to be up high on top of a horse, who is happy to do whatever I want.*

The unaccustomed stock saddle feels strangely enclosing with its protective knee pads pressing against her thighs, yet somehow also feels reassuring, as if it holds her close, like a hug.

'Ok now?' Ben appears leading a dapple-grey mare with a dainty dished head, large velvety eyes and a flowing mane.

Ria has no need to say anything. Her smile is enough.

With practised ease Ben is in the saddle and heading towards the gate. The gate opened, he ushers Ria through.

'I'll do the gates today but be warned. In future, we'll share gate duty.'

'And just keep an eye out for Bess and Roly here,' he says pointing at the two kelpie dogs darting ahead. 'They should keep out of your way, but with Roly…,' he shrugs, his meaning clear.

'Roly, short for Roland, but who would use that name? He's only a pup and may be a good worker in time, but he's still a bit wild and rolls in anything disgusting. He's one of Bess' pups that no one would buy from me. Probably there's a reason for that. I'm hoping he might learn from her, but so far he's showing very little sign of improvement.'

Escorted by the enthusiastic farm dogs they leave the stable yards and head away from the house following a farm track onto which the various paddocks open. Ben explains that the farm is linked by a series of laneways that provide easy access to the sheep and cattle yards and to the stables.

'It makes it easier with the laneways. When we need to move stock we just open the gate in their paddock and the gate in the paddock we want them to go, shunt them into the laneway and the stock pretty much do the rest. Sometimes I think they might be just like us and enjoy a change of scenery, or maybe they are keen to try something different to eat. Whatever the reason, they're rarely any trouble to move.'

As they ride along at a sedate walk Ben keeps on talking, telling Ria about where they are heading, what is in each paddock and his plans for the stock. But Ria is only half listening. Her entire being is focussed on the long-forgotten thrill of being at ease with a horse, moving in rhythm with his movements, smelling his sweet grassy smell, listening to the jingle of the bit, the snort and shake of the head, and delighting in the whole experience.

With a rush, she turns to Ben and interrupts him in mid-sentence. 'Thank you, Ben. And thank you Tonka too, of course,' she says, leaning forward and patting the muscled, coppery, gleaming neck. 'This is amazing. You've no idea how much I've missed this. Not that my horse-riding experience was ever anything like this,' Ria says waving her hand around. Tonka's ears flicker, but he shows no other reaction to her sudden movement.

'In my teens, I rode at a riding school – weekly lessons – that sort of thing. But never in surroundings like this and the horses were never as good as Tonka. Already I can see that he is far superior to anything I have ever ridden before.'

'Yes, he is,' says Ben complacently. 'Fancy a trot? Fidget here certainly could go one.'

'Oh, I don't know. It's been so long.' All of a sudden, Ria is filled with doubt about her ability to stay on.

'Well you have to try again at some stage, and why not now? Just give him a little squeeze into a lope. You'll be fine. Trust me.'

And so she was. At Ben's urging they went faster into a full trot and then moved into a canter, which as Ben had described it earlier was just like being in an armchair, or to Ria's way of thinking, like sitting on a rocking horse.

Tonka, she decides is a prince of a horse. And with such manners. As soon as she thought it was time to slow down, he responded, slowing to a trot and then to an ambling walk.

'How did he do that?' Ria glows in delight. 'How did he know I was ready to slow down? Is this precious horse psychic?'

'No, just good mannered – or possibly tired. He's not so fit at the moment,' says Ben, trying to convince his horse to do likewise, as she prances and sidles, tossing head and mane and flicking her tail in frustration.

'Unlike this girl, who sees no reason to walk when you can canter or even gallop. But if you gave him the signals that you wanted to slow down, like leaning back, he will know that means slow down. Lean forward or shorten your reins and he will know you plan to speed up. As does madam here,' he says, giving a demonstration. A slight lean forward and shortening of reins and Fidget is off trotting and clearly wanting to go faster. Ben slows, then halts her and then, all a prance, Fidget returns to Ria and Tonka.

'I spend a lot of time trying to convince Fidget that there is more to life than cantering. Some days she believes me. Most days she requires a lot of persuading. It's the Arab in her – she is bred for speed and she knows it!'

They continue to ride along the laneway, until Ben opens a gate to the right and gestures Ria through.

'Here. We'll go into this paddock. No stock in here at the moment, so we can leave the gate open. There's a bit of a rise further on and from there a great view of the village. Are you ready?'

Seeing Ria's nod Ben gathers his reins and sets off at a very slow canter, much to Fidget's disgust as evidenced by snorting and head tossing. Tonka has no trouble keeping up with an extended trot. Neck and neck they arrive at the rise, all out of breath and exhilarated. Reins loosened both horses take the opportunity to graze, eagerly yanking at the long grass before them.

'There. See over there,' says Ben pointing down the valley. 'You can see the village. The mighty *Kings Vale*. Once it was a village full of workers that supported this property and the surrounding properties. These days it is a sort of satellite village. Many folks that live there work in Canberra but want the country lifestyle. Can't say I blame them. Who'd want to live in town?'

Some distance away Ria can see a cluster of roofs, two church towers and a mass of greenery. Only seen for the first time the day before yesterday, but no longer feeling strange to her. In the foreground, paddocks in various shades of gold and green. Some she sees have been mowed short. Ben explains that they were the hay fields. Fields where the hay has been cut some months before, baled and is now in storage in the hay shed ready for use come winter. White fluff balls punctuate the cropped fields.

'Sheep,' Ben explains. 'Eating the stubble and fertilising the field with their droppings.'

'Some of the grass is a browny colour and some different shades of green,' Ria observes. 'Why're they different?'

Ben twinkles at her.

'City girl! You're so ignorant! Now I won't turn this into a lecture on farming. But they're all different colours for a reason. See that paddock by the creek there – the flattish land with the dark green pasture.' His hand points back towards the direction of the house. 'That's our lucerne paddock. We've already baled that paddock some time ago. You know, made hay. Anyway, what with the autumn rain and the recent warm weather, it has started to regrow and that's why it is such a rich green colour with the new growth. We'll probably just graze the sheep out on it in the next week or so. Over there.' He now points back towards the stables. 'That's the improved pasture – specially planted with non-native grasses. That paddock is being spelled – having a rest I mean and is also regrowing because of the recent rain. We moved the cattle out of it just before the rain. You can see them over there on the golden coloured grass. That is grass that has matured and dried out. They'll eat that and find the regrowth closer to the ground. Those girls are in calf and will be calving in the next few months. We want them in good condition, but not too good. So, they're now in a large paddock with a bit of a walk whenever they're thirsty to get to the water. Cows need their exercise too!'

As they smile at each other Ria senses that the time is now right to ask a few more questions. Taking a deep breath, she tries to explain why this is so important to her.

'Ben, I know this sounds weird. But until I read the letter mum left me after she died, I didn't know you or your mum – or Kitty – even existed. So, the last few days have felt incredibly surreal. You know, leaving crowded, grimy Sydney and arriving at this wonderland full of space and beauty. So much to take in – the amazing historic house, such beautiful natural surroundings and perfect animals.'

This all said while patting Tonka, who busily focussing on the grass before him, pays her no attention, apart from a flicker of his ears.

'I feel like I'm in some sort of fairy tale. Where I've woken in an alternate reality full of beauty and with a family I always wished I had. Don't get me wrong. I loved my mum and Penny is amazing, but to have a cousin and a real aunt – well, that is a wish come true.' With a breaking voice Ria continues, 'But I don't understand. Why? Who are you? I know so little. I don't even know who else belongs to this family or where they are. What happened? Why didn't mum talk to your mum, or even mention your existence to me.'

Ben looks puzzled.

'I don't know either. But believe me. I'm very happy to have a cousin, and I know mum is so pleased you are here. When she received your letter, she was delighted. You should have seen her face. In fact, the first thing she did was to come running out to the shed to find me and to tell me the news. I think somehow, she must have already known that you existed. For she kept saying: 'I never thought this day would come when I could actually meet her.'

'Over and over, she said that, like she couldn't believe it was finally happening. If you want to know more you probably need to ask mum. I can't tell you much, as I for one, never knew you existed, until the day mum got your letter.'

'Kitty?' Ria asks.

'Ah, Kitty. That's another story. I suppose as part of this family you need to know.'

Taking a deep breath Ben starts to explain.

'She's my sister – my little sister. About 20 now, I think. Yeah, that'd be right. I was 6 when she was born. Still remember that. Called after mum, but we all called her Kitty to avoid confusion. You would have loved her. Everyone did – funny, sparkling, intelligent, but so restless. Like Fidget here. She could never sit still for long. Always wanting to do something else. Never could finish a book, a game or a conversation. Like quicksilver she was.'

Like my mother, Ria thinks to herself.

'Anyway, the long and the short of it was she ran away. In her final year of high school, it was. Two years ago. She had a blazing row with mum and dad about something mindless and left in the middle of the night, taking all the cash she could find. No note, no forwarding address. Nothing. Mum and dad were sick with worry. We searched. Put out notices, tried all her friends – but couldn't find her or any news about where she'd gone. In the end, the Police told us there was nothing further we could do. They'd tracked her down in Sydney. They said she was living rough. Said she was ok and getting some charity assistance but wanted to have nothing to do with us. The Police said all we could do was to wait until Kitty chose to make contact.'

'Mum and dad nearly went mad with the grief. Kitty was dad's little princess, you see. Mum shut up Kitty's room. It's still shut up. Waiting for her to return I guess. But it's a big house and one less room to clean is no loss.'

Ben smiles sadly and continues: 'They tried to sell old Tonk, but I wouldn't let them. Told mum I would look after him. After that mum threw herself into the business and tried to act as if Kitty had never happened. And dad......' Ben stops talking and looks miserably out before him, across the valley towards the village.

Ria dreads asking, but finds she has to know.

'And your dad?'

'He killed himself soon after.'

At this Ria feels the air sucked out of her and her very being becoming paralysed. Why did she feel she had to pry and inflict further pain on this person who already she is coming to like?

Ria draws in a deep breath and finds herself saying 'I'm sorry, I'm so sorry', over and over again.

Ben smiles at her sadly, takes up the reins then nudges his horse forward heading back in the direction they came.

'Don't be sorry. It was a story you needed to know. As I said earlier, this is not the wonderful fairy tale it appears on the surface. Sure, we live in the beautiful home and appear to lack for nothing, but we are damaged people and I hope the damage doesn't extend to you or infect you. Or maybe it is something that is already in all our DNA? Maybe that is why your mother kept you away from us

– to shield you somehow. Yet I'm glad you're here with us now and I know mum is also. No pressure, but I do wonder if she might see you as someone to fill our Kitty's shoes, to replace her lost daughter?'

'You know you said it felt like a fairy tale being here,' Ben continues. 'Well, I'm not sure that is correct. Some days I wonder if we are living in a Greek tragedy, with no hope for a happy ending, but doomed to descend into madness and despair.'

His words fall into the silence between them. Ria is at a loss as to how to respond and focusses instead on moving her horse forward.

As they head for home Ria's mind is full of what she has just heard. Pondering, disassembling and reassembling in various combinations – but it still doesn't make sense. Nothing she has heard explains her mother's actions.

With her experience as a nurse, and especially in her latest position in the paediatric ward, Ria is all too aware that life can be full of tragedy, and sometimes certain families attract more than their fair share. Could Ben be correct when he said that this family was doomed?

Despite what has just been revealed, in some way she feels a strange satisfaction in knowing another part of the story, for she is sure there is still more waiting to be discovered. If nothing else, Ria now feels that she is developing some awareness of the true nature of the family to which she belongs.

Perhaps it is the resilience of youth or perhaps it is the beauty that surrounds her, but Ria cannot help but feel optimistic this day. As she rocks in rhythm to her horse's gait and soaks up the serenity of the vista before her – pasture, woodland and those stone buildings drawing closer with each step, she feels the need to share her feelings with Ben, with the hope that maybe it might also help to ease his pain.

'Thank you, Ben. And thank you for being so open with me. I can only guess how hard it must be to speak of these painful times. But somehow, I feel that if this family thing is going to work and I can be a support to your mum and to you, it is important that there be no secrets – well not too many,' she corrects herself.

Seeing Ben's slight smile, she rushes on: 'and thanks: to you, and Tonka and Miss Fidget for the ride today. I can't tell you how much I loved it. Can we do it again? Soon? Or maybe once my muscles recover. I'm sure to be a cripple tomorrow!'

With that Ben's smile spreads and she finds herself gazing in awe at this beautiful, although rather scruffy, man beside her.

'My pleasure. And Tonka's too. He gets bored being stuck in the paddock without a friend. He loved Kitty so – and judging by his perfect behaviour with you today – I think he might also like you. Just ignore the muscles. They'll get used to it very quickly, especially if we ride every day. You can help me with the stock work. There's also something else you can help me with – very soon actually. I'll show you when we get back.'

Despite her entreaties to know more, Ben just smiles mysteriously and apart from muttering: 'You'll see,' he says nothing further.

Once back at the stables, Ria busies herself unsaddling Tonka and putting his gear away in the tack shed. Ben directs her to the wash bay where she gives Tonka a quick hose and then releases him into the paddock. But Tonka doesn't walk away. He stays by her, nuzzling Ria's pockets.

'The old rogue,' says Ben, leading Fidget into the paddock. 'He's after a treat.' Reaching into his pocket Ben unearths a carrot.

'There, give him half of this. Fidget can have the other half.'

Ria snaps the carrot in half. Then holding out her hand flat, she laughs when Tonka's velvety lips tickle her hand, as he daintily takes the carrot into his mouth.

'Come on,' says Ben once both horses are dismissed. 'This way,' and he leads her back to the stables and towards the end stable. Inside there is another horse busily eating hay. Ria can see that this horse is different to Fidget and Tonka. Taller, finer – a bay in colour, with black mane, tail and legs – and an enormous bulging middle.

'This is Trixie, one of my father's mares. She's a stock horse. Dad was keen on breeding stock horses. The others are out in that paddock, where we just released the horses.

Ben stands by her side and gently strokes her neck, all the while whispering into the horse's ear, which flickers as she listens. Ben runs his hands down her back and continues, 'It's probably obvious. But she's in foal and doesn't have too long to go. Old Trixie here has had many foals in the past and we really thought she wouldn't fall this time. I let her run with the neighbour's stallion last year thinking the chances of her falling in foal were zip, and then blow me down if it didn't happen straight away!'

He pats Trixie on the neck and moves away, taking Ria by the arm and leading her out of the stable.

'There. Let's leave her in peace. She hasn't got long to go now. That's why I've moved her away from the herd the other day. Now all we need to do is to keep an eye on her. Hopefully Trixie will take care of the rest and won't need any help from us. But you never know. Each time can be different. Helped with any deliveries before?' Ben asks with a quizzical expression.

'Only human ones,' confesses Ria.

'Well, animals do it so much better,' he laughs. 'Much less complaining. And the animal baby can walk almost straight away. A vast improvement on us humans!'

He adds, 'But you can help me with Trixie when her time comes. That is, if you want?'

Of course Ria wants.

Chapter Six

As they amble back to the house, plans are made to go for a further ride the next day – Ria's muscles permitting. Before they reach the house, Ben diverts them to a cluster of sheds which he tells her are the farm machinery sheds – and to one special shed towards the back, which he describes as his *art shed*. The *art shed* is made from rusty corrugated iron and attached to a much larger and more decrepit shed. He opens the doors with a flourish and points to the creation before them. There Ria can see a construction of metal – curved on itself and, in parts, twisted and curved away like a series of contorted loops. For a moment Ria finds herself unsure of what to say. The curves she sees, at once so regular and expected, yet the twists and contortions speak to her of an internal tension and an inherent conflict. As she struggles to put these concepts into words, Ben's excited reaction amazes her.

'That's exactly what I was trying to say. The beauty of the curves hides within it the drama of unexpected tension. As if it is all going to explode apart at any given moment. A bit like an analogy for life. You know, just when you think all is ok on the surface, then it all falls apart. A bit like our family I guess.' Ben smiles faintly, and then adds. 'Perhaps I should call it *Family Life?*'

With building enthusiasm Ben explains that the sculpture is almost complete, and details how he hopes to show it at a regional exhibition in the spring. That is, if he gets time to finish it by then.

'The farm work gets in the way. Animals don't wait their turn you know.'

In response to Ria's prompting, Ben tells her about his art studies. How he had studied sculpture at art school and completed his degree but had to return home to help his parents manage when it all fell in a heap following Kitty's disappearance. And then after his father's death, there was then no question of his leaving. His mother needed him to help run the farm. His art had to take a back seat. Sure, they have some assistance – the farm hand and seasonal contractors help a lot, but Ben feels he has had to step into his father's shoes and be a combined manager, extra farm hand and general dogs body. In saying this Ben shrugs, trying to look like it doesn't matter, but Ria can see it clearly does. She rests her hand on his arm.

'If I can support you in any way please let me,' she says.

'Are you kidding? Your just being here is great. You have no idea. I just hope you can stay for a while?'

'It's possible. Maybe. I've taken leave from work. I had so much owing to me and Penny is happy for me to stay away for a while. She thought I needed to have a break from home – away from all those sad memories about my mum I guess. Let's just see how we go. You might change your mind once you get to know me better!'

They walk slowly back to the house, each lost in their own thoughts. Back at the house Ben leaves her in the kitchen, saying he has chores to do.

Ria settles at the kitchen table, alone except for her thoughts, which continue to puzzle over the mystery that is her family. Using the kitchen telephone, she rings Penny. Speaking softly, as she is not sure if anyone is nearby, she updates Penny on the events of the last two days – the happy confusion of the open garden and the wonder of that morning's ride. She explains that she might stay a while, so long as Penny can manage.

'Stay as long as you like. You need a break after all that has happened. I'm glad you're enjoying yourself. How is your new family?'

At this Ria describes her interaction with her aunt and cousin.

'Do you know why mum never mentioned them? It all seems very strange that I have this family living not that far away from Sydney and yet I know nothing about them.'

Silence on the other end of the phone. It's almost as if Penny is collecting her thoughts and then censoring them before she speaks, searching for the right words to say.

'My dear. I'm sorry, but I have no idea why your mother behaved as she did. When she arrived at my front door all those years ago, unannounced and unexpected, she was quite distraught. She refused to say anything about what had happened – just that she was never going back. She let me contact her parents to say she was safe, but she refused to talk to them. I was in a quandary as you might expect. You see I was very close to your grandmother – that's why they asked me to be your mother's godmother. I felt my loyalties lay with them, yet I couldn't turn Bianca away. So reluctantly I concluded that I had no choice but to let her stay. I didn't grill her. I just let her recover. She was in quite a state you see, and she needed rest and feeding. Looking back, I realise she must have been pregnant by then, but she didn't mention it. I didn't notice it until her condition became really obvious. You know baggy clothes can disguise a lot - and I guess it didn't cross my mind your mother could be pregnant – she was still a child to me. She was probably almost five months along by the time I noticed. I suppose her pregnancy had something to do with her running away from home, but Bianca never said if that was the case. And once you were born, we both looked to the future.'

Ria could hear Penny draw a deep breath before she continues. Obviously, the events of so long ago still deeply affect her.

'I once asked her if she wanted to take you back home and show you to your grandparents. Bianca was adamant she would never go home and we never spoke of it after. You see your mother made it clear to me that I was not to discuss the matter again. You remember how fierce she could be when someone spoke to her about something she didn't want to hear? Well, she was like that then. Maybe I was also a little bit selfish. I didn't want to be the cause of her leaving and taking you with her. I so loved my new family.'

Ria ends the call reluctantly. The sound of Penny's voice – so much a part of her life up to now – grounding and reassuring her.

She slowly replaces the receiver and stares across the kitchen lost in thoughts of her childhood.

In many ways, it was a different childhood to that experienced by her peers. The only child of a single parent with an absent – no, make that unknown - father, her childhood should have been sad and lonely. Yet when she looks back on her childhood, Ria can only recall a time of constant chaos, love and laughter. Adored by her mother and Penny, Ria never lacked for affection and never felt the need for another parent. In the early years of her life, when Penny took in young university students as boarders, there was always a young person or two to fuss over her, whenever her mother or Penny were busy. Always someone on hand to indulge her, read her a story or just tell her how wonderful she was. No. Ria had no memories of ever being alone or unloved. Then later on, once her mother had the bright idea of converting Penny's house into bed and breakfast accommodation, her life resembled any day on the set of a comic soap opera on television - a sort of *Fawlty Towers*. With an endless array of characters arriving to stay and countless catastrophes, the lives of her fellow school students seemed incredibly dull by comparison.

No. She didn't lack for anything, Ria tells herself. Her mother, wise and clever in all things, must have had good reasons for keeping her secrets to herself. Maybe, if Ria stays here long enough, she will find out why her mother behaved as she did. Or, maybe, a little voice in her head interjects, maybe she will never know, and she will just have to learn to live with that. But can she?

Chapter Seven

Sometime later her aunt and Shelley appear. Follow up calls now completed and further appointments made with potential customers, they both enter the room full of chatter about these achievements, and about the plans they have just finalised for the next event – another wedding.

As her aunt explains, for most events the customer is signed up to a full package where services from external providers are included. Caterers, marquee hire, glassware and cutlery are all arranged and included in the package. Aunt Kat says she has been doing this for years and has a panel of contractors who are reliable and know the venue.

'It makes it so much easier doing it this way. Why worry about providing these services, when there are experts who can do so? All we generally have to do, is make sure whichever part of the house or garden is to be used looks amazing. The florist does the flower arrangements – even in the toilets – although we do need to make sure they're clean. It may sound like we don't have to do much, but it's still a fair bit. We still have oversight – to make sure all is properly organised and ready to go when the customer wants it and to make sure the event runs smoothly. That's why I only use businesses I can trust. It all has to be perfect – so we can maintain our reputation.'

She continues: 'and this time of the year is such a pain. Autumn. Don't look so surprised Ria. You'll understand soon enough. You'll see what I mean for sure with the next function - a wedding. Well, they want to exchange vows in the house, gather for drinks in the courtyard, and then have the reception in a marquee nearby. The marquee is the easy bit. But one of us will be blowing leaves away in the courtyard, right up until just before the guests arrive. With our luck leaves will fall on the bride and groom! Well, I have warned them. They've said that will be charming. But the reality may not be so when damp leaves mess up the bride's precious hairstyle. Believe me there is nothing worse than an unhappy customer and even though we occasionally get those, they're best to be avoided. So that is why the leaf blower will be in full use before the next wedding!'

As they sit down at the table to each enjoy a coffee, Ria tells them about the delight that was her ride this morning and how, muscles cooperating, she hopes she can repeat the experience tomorrow.

'I do hope you can, Ria dear,' her aunt says. 'It's so good for Ben to have some company. I hope that horse you rode behaved?'

'He was just perfect,' Ria gushes in her enthusiasm. 'I have never ridden such a beautiful horse with amazing manners.'

'Yes, Kitty did a good job with him. They were champions at the local show many times you know.'

With that her aunt's face clouds over and she reaches with trembling hands for her coffee. At Shelley's anxious look Ria searches desperately for a new topic of conversation and launches into a description of her phone call to Penny.

She turns to Shelley saying: 'I spoke to Penny about you coming to visit and she says she would love you to stay for as long as you would like. I'll give you her phone number and some directions and then you can make contact once you decide when you'll arrive. There's always someone there – Penny or the manager – to greet guests you know. You can have my room. Sorry about the mess I left it in. Penny will give you a door key, so you can come and go as you like.'

In her soft Irish brogue Shelley utters her thanks. Then with a rising inflexion as her excitement mounts, she starts to list all the things she wants to see and do while she is in Sydney.

Aunt Kat holds up her hand.

'Whoa, Shelley, no more! Go make your booking. Ring Penny and start packing. Clearly, we will get no more sense from you today. Such excitement. Anyone would think you were glad to leave us!'

Shelley's horrified expression and protestations make Ria and her aunt both laugh out loud.

'Go! Off with you child, before you make me wet my knickers! I can't laugh like this for too long you know. I'm too old.'

Aunt Kat wipes the tears from her eyes and then shunts Shelley from the room. Turning back to Ria with the smile fading from her eyes, she gazes tenderly at her niece.

'Let me get a proper look at you now. I know you have been here two days now, but we have yet to have a proper chat or even a moment's peace together. My apologies for your rushed introduction to this family. It's often like this I'm afraid.'

Ria's flustered disclaimer is brushed aside.

'No. It's us who have been at fault. No sooner had you arrived than you were put to work. I'd like to say that won't continue, but that would make me a liar – especially now Shelley is going on holiday. Well, you wouldn't want to be bored, would you?'

Ria finds herself now being closely examined by her aunt.

'Mmmm. Let me see. Yes, I think you do have the look of your mother. Same colour eyes as her – cornflower blue with a hint of green – rather unusual I would expect. And your hair is somehow a bit lighter. Your mum's hair was darker I recall – maybe hers was more in the coppery, chestnut toning's and yours is a red gold. Very pretty I must say. Yours is darker than Ben's but not as dark as your mother's hair.'

'You're not as tall as me, but then your mum was shorter. But I think you are strong – maybe stronger than your mother?'

She looks questioningly at Ria, who nods.

'Yes, I would expect you would have to be – being a nurse and all that. Not just strong physically, but also strong emotionally. Like how you have taken the last few months in your stride. So much seems to have happened to you, yet I think you have managed to cope. Your mum's sudden illness, her death and finding out about us. Yet here you are – unflappable. That says a lot about you and from what I recall so very different to your mother.'

Noticing her aunt seems to be relaxing again into the conversation, Ria now seizes the opportunity to dive in.

'Tell me about my mum. She never said anything much about growing up at *Kings Vale.*'

Now that's a slight exaggeration, Ria thinks to herself. *Well, it's a big exaggeration, given her mother never said anything at all about growing up in the village.*

Her aunt smiles.

'It was all so long ago. You know our father was the local doctor?'

Ria nods. *Did she know this? No – not at all.*

'We lived in a lovely old rambling house in the village. The doctor's surgery to one side – accessible by a separate path. Your grandmother helped in the surgery. She was a trained nurse you see – just like you. Maybe it's a family thing?' Kat looked across at her niece with eyebrows raised. Ria smiles but says nothing. How could she express an opinion about an unknown family member?

'Anyway, they both died quite some time ago, but I think they would've loved you.'

Her aunt pauses, clearly lost in memories, sighs, shakes her head as if to toss unwelcome thoughts away, and then continues:

'There were only two of us. Your mother was the baby – four years younger than me - I think. Cute as a button and didn't she know it! And spoilt rotten by us all. We all indulged her. It was hard not to. She was such a sweetie – with those long coppery curls, pale, pale skin – like alabaster it was, and those amazing eyes – she really was irresistible, especially when she turned on the charm! Always in a rush and so restless. She became more so as she got older. You know, thinking back on it I can see it was obvious she never fitted into country life. Allergic to grass and horses, and so easily sunburnt. It's no surprise that she couldn't wait to get away.'

She sighs and takes a sip of the now tepid coffee.

'In fact, it's a wonder she stayed here for as long as she did.'

Chapter Eight

1975 – Bianca

Sometimes Bianca wondered if she had been adopted or swapped at birth at the district hospital.

Many times, she felt that she did not belong to this family. Everything about them was wrong. Her parents, so consumed with the health and well-being of everyone in the village, but never noticing her. Her big sister married now for two years and still starting every sentence with: 'Mick says', or 'Mick thinks' or 'Mick this' or 'Mick that' – as if he was a god! And these days her sister, totally besotted with her newborn son, was acting as if a baby had never been born before. In fact, the entire family, apart from her that is, were also behaving in this silly manner. They'd all gone gaga.

Poor mite. Not only was it his bad luck to be born into this family, but his parents had also lumped him with a revolting name. Benedict! Didn't this family ever learn? Bianca for one moment felt a brief sense of pity for this red-faced slobbering infant. Giving him that name will toughen him up for sure. She could already think of all the names the inventive kids at the village school would call him. After all, hadn't she experienced that herself years ago, until it stopped once she punched them out?

Bianca the wanker, she had been called, accompanied by matching gestures. Well, she sorted them out. Now they just called her: *Stuck up bitch*.

She couldn't wait until she finished school later this year, and could get away from small town life, where daily conversation was focussed on the weather, the rainfall, the local footie competition and now – this squalling baby, who seemed to be this month's number one story.

Usually nothing happened in this place except for the weekly rotation of school, church and the footy. But tonight, it would be different. For once there was something to look forward to. Tonight, was the night of the annual village ball. Being held in the old memorial hall – built to commemorate those who gave their lives in World War One it was usually a shabby, draughty, weatherboard affair. Yet tonight, decorated with flowers and shimmering lights, the hall would be stylish and sophisticated and so different to its everyday humdrum existence. The ball – fancy dress of course - was the highlight in the social calendar for those living near and far. Not that there was much competition. Only the occasional bachelor and spinsters' ball, but she had never been allowed to attend those! Too debauched, or so her parents said.

But tonight, she would be attending – with her parents. Her first ever ball. No partner to take her there, but then again, there was no one in this hick town that she could bear to be seen with, let alone go out with. She didn't mind being partnerless, as she would be able to sit with her mum and dad, and with Mick, her brother-in-law. Kat said she wouldn't go. The baby at four weeks of age was too young to leave. *Well, her loss*, thought Bianca.

Her first ball! There was no way she was going to miss it!

The theme for tonight's event was *Charleston and Gangster Times*. Her mum had found her an outfit, something she had worn years ago and was almost teary when she saw Bianca swishing around in this 1920's Flappers style outfit.

'I remember when I wore that years ago to a fancy-dress ball. It takes me right back. Here, let me tie back your hair. No bob for you, but maybe we can try to restrain your curls somehow, perhaps tie a ribbon through and around them somehow – sort of like a hairband - so they lie a bit flatter? And here put these on,' as she hands Bianca several strands of long fake pearls. 'There, that should do it. Beautiful!'

Bianca, staring at her reflection in the full-length mirror, is also amazed. A stranger stares back at her, resplendent in a dress fringed with glittering bugle beads.

Not bad, she thinks to herself. The black of the dress makes her skin appear even paler, almost translucent. Her fiery hair, almost tamed and her eyes outlined with black eyeliner, now glow sapphire.

So wasted on this stinking place, she thinks.

Yet some time later she changes her mind. Bolstered by several glasses of champagne, furtively consumed when her parents were not looking, she decides that the village is not so bad after all. She has danced every dance with a variety of young men – some known to her and some total strangers. All tell her how stunning she is tonight, and for that reason she finds herself liking them all, and not objecting to matching their drinks, glass for glass

Over in the corner she can see her parents deep in conversation, apparently enjoying the evening in their own peculiar way. Bianca starts to head across to them when she is waylaid by Mick, her sister's husband. She stumbles and then grabs him by the arm. After all, she has known him forever. He is like a brother to her. He steadies her.

'Bianca. Careful there. Having fun? Looks like you've had a few!'

Bianca's response is a hiccough delivered with a slightly glassy stare.

'More than a few it would seem. Hang onto me. I'll tell your folks I'll get you home. I need to get home to Kat anyway, so I can drop you on my way past. Sit down here. I'll be right back.'

Bianca slumps down into the proffered chair. She is vaguely aware of voices. Mick's deeper tones assuring someone – her parents she supposes – that he will get her home and not to worry. She tries to focus on the dance floor, but for some reason it keeps moving. She looks up at the dancing figures, which appear to be all a wobble and a blur. The music, a tune that she vaguely recognises, vibrates right into her very being. She senses a person drawing near – an arm pulling her up, drawing her close and then gently pushing her out the door.

'Come on princess. Home to bed with you. I don't think you're going to feel too good in the morning and probably won't remember too much.'

She feels herself being pushed into the car seat, senses the rocking motion as the car moves forward and lapses into a type of sleep, where she is still vaguely aware of the car radio playing some pop tune that is somehow familiar. The movement ceases. Her door opens and she feels the cool evening air on her face, pulling her to consciousness, but not quite.

Arms reach around her, pulling her out of the car.

Words murmuring in her ear. 'Come on sweetheart. A bit of co-operation wouldn't go astray. That's right – one step in front of the other. Let's get you to bed.'

She feels herself being laid onto her bed and then gently, very gently, hands undoing her dress and somehow pulling the dress off her. This seems to require some effort from her. When she is urged to lift her arms or wiggle free she does so. The hands run along her body and she feels her bra being loosened and then removed. The hands gently rub across her nipples, cupping her tiny breasts one after the other. She feels sucking at her nipples and the sensation of a corresponding tightening in her pelvis.

She hears a voice murmuring but does not register the reality of the voice or what it is saying. Afterwards when Bianca berates herself for letting herself be so vulnerable, she wonders why she did not object then and there and push Mick away. Later, she cannot understand why she let this happen to her. And yet, thinking back to her vague recollection of the events and what followed, she recalls how in her drunken haze it felt not quite real, but more like a dream. In that dream her young body responded, as it was made to do, to touch and pressure. And in her dreamlike state, when all sense of right and wrong was suspended or displaced by the alcohol she'd consumed, she was unable to do anything but react to those sensations. That is, until the moment when she felt overwhelming pressure and accompanying pain, as she felt a sensation of something enormous being forced into a very tight space that was part of her. At this point, any feelings of pleasure immediately evaporated, and her only instinct was to squirm away from the source of this pain. Even in her inebriated state her body knew pain when it felt it. She bucked and tried to move away from this sensation. But hands held her firmly, bodyweight pressed down on her fragile bones and movement was impossible. The hurt intensified as the battering ram pushed through. Too late she became fully aware of what was happening. Yet in her awareness she froze. Finally, able to comprehend what was happening to her and by whom, but unable to move.

She now understands that her brother-in-law is the one pushing her firmly into the mattress and forcing himself into her. She cries, but even as she does so she understands it is hopeless. His eyes in the face looming above her, are closed, as he pounds away, with each movement ripping at both her body and her heart.

All the time she can hear him say:

'So good. I knew you would feel so good. So tight, so perfect a young filly, not like your sister, that old broodmare back at home. Don't squirm. I know you wanted it – you little tart. Looking for it tonight, weren't you?'

The pumping accelerates and with one final thrust it is over.

Bianca just lies there. Eyes closed and hoping he will leave. She hears him zip up his pants, cover her with a quilt and then whisper in her ear.

'This is just between us. You hear? You don't want your sister to know you led me on do you? What's a man to do when you had it all on offer tonight? And maybe I might be back for more sometime. If you make yourself available, I might just keep our little secret as well.'

Sometime later she stirs and tries so sit up. Her arms feel sore where he held her down. There will be bruises in the morning. Her thighs are bloodied and throb, as if they have been ripped apart – which, she thinks, maybe they have been. She stumbles to the bathroom, steps into the shower and stands there under the flowing water – as hot as she can make it – scrubbing, rubbing and washing over and over – all the while, her tears adding extra moisture.

Back in bed, now beyond tears, she contemplates the disaster that was that night. The young woman who had twirled in the mirror only a few hours before, innocently admiring her beauty, is no longer. All that remains is a broken and bruised wreck.

She hears her parents arrive home, their shared laughter echoing down the hallway. She wonders how she will ever manage to act as if nothing has happened when she next sees them, for she knows there is no point in her explaining what has just happened. No-one will believe her. They would not accept as true, a story of an assault on her by someone like Mick. A pillar of society, the son of the largest landowner in the region – no, it was unbelievable.

If the unthinkable occurred and she was believed and she knows that would be most unlikely – after all it would be his word against hers – then what outcome would she achieve? Shame for her and her family, unhappiness for her sister and it would still not alter her physical and mental pain.

No, she tells herself. She must lock the pain away, pretend it had never happened or had happened to some other girl and keep as far away from Mick as possible. And make sure he never gets the opportunity to get near her again.

Somehow Bianca manages to fall asleep. It is not until mid-morning that her mother disturbs her rest. Opening the bedroom door a crack, and poking her head in she whispers:

'Good morning miss. You've had a late night then. Are you ready to get up?'

Bianca rolls over and makes a pretence of burrowing under the blankets. She doesn't want her mother to look too closely. To her mother's inquiry she grunts that she might get up soon.

'No dear, don't rush. Your dad and I are off up to see your sister. We told her we would pop in and give her a hand with the baby. Unless you want to join us?'

Never thinks Bianca. *Never again!* She tries to respond politely.

'No, not at all. A bit tired. I might just take it easy and I'll see you later.'

She lies in bed until she hears her parent's car reverse out the driveway, then dragging herself upright she climbs out of her bed. Her body feels even worse than she expected. Her head aching with what she assumes is her first hangover. Feet sore from all the dancing last night. Her thighs and her very being complain from Mick's assault. In the mirror, she can see bruises already marking her upper arms and inner thighs. Turning her face resolutely away she reaches for a loose, long-sleeved smock which, worn over pedal pushers, will cover all evidence of the assault from her parent's gaze.

The bedlinen, she strips and bundles into the washing machine. At least if questioned by her mother she can say that her periods came early. Not that she will notice. Her mother never pays any attention to her anyway.

Sometime later, in the kitchen she sits at the table, hands clasped around a mug of tea as she stares vacantly at the clutter on the table before her. Over and over Bianca wonders what to do. Yet no answer comes to her. All she knows is that she must pretend that the events of last night never happened. She was often being told, sometimes by others rather spitefully, that she was a bit of an actress. Well, now she tells herself, she must act in the hardest role she has ever had in her life. Her acting must be the best she has ever done.

Her sister must never know what happened last night. For if she did, it would surely break her heart?

Over the following days and weeks Bianca carries on as if all is well, even if on the inside she feels like she is falling apart.

She wonders why no one notices that she is a changed person. Surely, she thinks, there must be a flashing sign above her head saying - *Alert, alert - beware damaged woman*. But no. Her parents act towards her just like they have always done – with loving, yet dismissive regard. Checking she has eaten, done her homework, mouthing platitudes as they go to bed, waking her up each morning and as they progress through the daily rituals. *Don't stay up too late now, hurry up or you'll miss the school bus*, and *eat your dinner – all your dinner miss!* She wonders if they even take one look at her. Perhaps this is just as well that they don't, as they fail to observe the dark circles under her eyes and her loss of weight.

Sometimes she wonders if a cardboard cut-out of herself could easily take her place, without causing her parents any concern.

One afternoon she arrives home from school to find her mother in the kitchen talking to Mick. The first time she has seen Mick since that awful night. She leaves her school bag by the door and goes to the sink for a glass of water – wondering if she can escape to her room without attracting comment.

Her mother greets her.

'Ah, Bianca. Just in time. I was going to make us a cuppa. Pop the kettle on will you love, while I go and bring in the washing. It's threatening rain, so I will make it quick.'

The back-door slams as her mother rushes out. Reaching for the kettle Bianca moves to the sink. Turning on the tap she stands at the kitchen sink, filling the kettle and staring out the window to the backyard.

She tenses, sensing Mick moving closer. His farmyard smells – scents of grass and animal – getting stronger. Then feeling him press hard up against her, both his hands reaching around her and holding her tight, her stomach pressed against the kitchen bench. She says nothing and continues to stare ahead, out the window.

His voice, whispering in her ear:

'Avoiding me, were you? Well, you can't you know. We're family after all.'

A hand sneaks under her school skirt, reaches under her knickers and massages her bum. He continues to whisper:

'Ah, but you're so gorgeous. You wicked girl. I think of you in the night. How good you felt. Your sister, well she won't let me near her. The baby - she says. But a man has his needs. Can't you feel how you make me feel?'

With that he presses even harder against her back and she can feel the bulk of his erection against her. She shudders with revulsion. But her shudders are misinterpreted. Mick, ever confident, mistakes it for lust and continues to whisper, pressing even harder, so she cannot move.

'You want it, don't you, you little devil. If only your mother wasn't here I would have you now, right here on the kitchen table. Now there's a thought. I will be back.'

She can hear her mother's steps approaching up the path, her voice speaking to the dog and the back door into the laundry opening with its usual squeak.

Mick's hand moves around to her front, briefly penetrates her, his ragged nail scratching her flesh, almost like he was deliberately branding her and causing her to flinch. Suddenly she is released as he moves back to the table to resume his seat, ready to greet her mother as if nothing had ever taken place. Sleek, complacent in his dominance over her, his only indication of triumph a darting, smirking glance in Bianca's direction.

Without a word Bianca resumes her task. The filled kettle now in place and switched on, she turns to her mother as she enters the room, telling her that she will get changed and get started on her homework.

'Of course, dear. I'll bring a cuppa to you.'

Mick stands.

'I'd better get moving too. Kat will be expecting me home, so I won't linger. I'll see you all later – maybe we could do something this weekend?'

Bianca can't help but shudder at the thought. She feels like a small insect trapped in a spider's web. She cannot escape. It is only a matter of time until Mick pounces and she doesn't know how she can avoid her fate.

Later that night, with sleep eluding her, Bianca concludes that the only solution rests with her. She must act. Clearly, she would like to inflict pain and injury on Mick, but to do so would only tear her family apart. That she cannot do. Momentarily she wonders if she should report her rape to the police, but she knows that she wouldn't be believed. Even if she was believed it would mean further pain for everyone – scandal with social exclusion for the entire family - and for what? No revenge for her. She cannot ever forget what happened. The pain will never go away. There is only one solution that she can think of and that is to get as far away from her home and her brother-in-law as possible.

After all she had never intended to stay here. She had always known that her life would start as soon as she left this place. Country life was never for her. For a moment, she thinks of the distress she will be inflicting on her parents and her sister – but that thought is resolutely pushed aside. Any other course of action she tells herself, would cause them even further distress. So what, that they will never know those alternatives? Only she will know that what she is about to do is for the best for everyone. Her parents. Kat and that baby Benedict, can get on with their lives without any interference from her or from Mick. For she knew that if she stayed he would not cease stalking her.

But where to go and how to get there? This occupies her thinking for some days and then inspiration strikes. She will go to Sydney and go to her godmother. At least go there in the first instance and that should give her enough time to plan her next step.

The very next day when her parents think she is headed off to school, Bianca with a duffle bag crammed with clothes, boards the train headed for Sydney. Only once the train starts to leave the station and moves forward, accelerating into speed, does she lean back into the seat and exhale a sigh of relief.

Her life can now begin.

Chapter Nine

2001 – Ria

It's Friday afternoon and Ria feels like she has been at *Kings View* for a lifetime. Already she has fallen in step with the daily rhythm of farm life. The early morning breakfast with her aunt and cousin, sometimes proceeding at a leisurely pace and sometimes rushed, depending upon the chores to be done that day. Over breakfast a discussion of what needs doing followed by a brief allocation of responsibilities. In Shelley's absence Ria finds herself helping her aunt with some of her tasks.

Spending time with her aunt, Ria discovers, is a welcome pleasure. So different from her sister, Ria's mother – not only physically different, but also so different in her behaviour. Whereas her mother was like a small, determined elf, vibrant and busy – all wild titian curls bobbing in time to her perpetual motion – her Aunt Kat is quietly purposeful, moving calmly and steadily from one task to the next. No drama and no temperament – just a steady progression through the day. On closer examination Ria observes the frown lines between her aunt's brows and the moments of quiet reflection that descend whenever her aunt feels she is unobserved. This makes her wonder if that calmness and steadiness is a façade that hides inner turmoil or a deep sorrow. On the other hand, the smiling face that she presents each morning could be evidence of a woman determined to keep up appearances despite the challenges in her life, or just happiness in seeing her much loved son and her newfound niece. Ria is just not sure which it is. With the loss of her own beloved mother so recently experienced and her suffering raw and painful like an open wound, Ria wishes she could derive some comfort from this newly found relative. But she senses that there is no comfort available to her from her aunt at this time, and that if anyone is to be the giver of comfort it is to be her. With that in mind Ria refrains from asking the endless questions that her mind has been busily formulating, as she focusses on trying to be a help to her aunt. Any further detail on what really happened to her uncle or to Kitty will just have to wait.

The highlight of each day, weather permitting, is the riding excursion with Ben. Tonka has come to recognise her as the welcome bearer of carrots and greets her approach with a whinny. In exchange for a tasty treat, he permits himself to be captured and led into the stable yard for saddling. With each day Ria's muscles become more accustomed to the exercise. This is a welcome relief as the agony suffered by her thighs after the first day's outing resulted in much distress to her and much hilarity for Ben.

Friday morning after breakfast finds Tonka and Ria tagging along behind Ben and a farmhand who could possibly be called Dave – Ria is not completely sure. It seems to be taken for granted that she already knows him. The task at hand is to move a mob of sheep into a new paddock. Ria is well aware that she is just along for the ride, as the dogs seem to be doing all the work. But she doesn't mind. The day is clear and warm and she is happy to delight in the experience of being outside with her now favourite horse. Tasked with bringing up the rear, her eyes are drawn to the sweep and curve of the sheltering hills, the vista of the multi-coloured paddocks before her and the swarming mass of sheep being cornered and moved through the gateway by the dogs and the two men. The image seems to her to be a quintessential rural scene, one that could be part of an epic movie about Australia. The noise: dogs barking, sheep baaing, men yelling, and whistling commands together with the swirls of dust disturbed by the panicked sheep, all contribute to the soundtrack and imagery of this epic.

All too soon the sheep are moved and settled into their new home – a welcome move it would appear, judging by the speed they settle into eating mode. Gate firmly secured Dave and dogs head away towards an outer paddock, with further tasks to do. Ben and Ria turn back for home, horses moving companionably side by side, their step now quickening as they sense that the homewards journey is before them.

'You really didn't need me, did you?'

'No. Not really. Nor me either. But I just wanted to check the condition of the sheep. Watching them move to a new paddock gives me a chance to see if any of them have foot problems you know. If they are moving freely then I know chances are they are ok. But any limping or signs of soreness is a signal that something needs to be checked. And you – well you need riding practice!'

'Come on! I'm not that bad, am I?'

'Ok for a city slicker I suppose. Show me how good you are – canter!'

And with that Ria urges Tonka into a canter. Not that he needs any urging. He knows the way home and is keen to get there. Canter extends into a gallop. Tonka and Fidget race neck and neck down the laneway. Just as Ria begins to wonder how she will stop Ben shouts:

'OK to slow down now?' Ben looks across at her with concern. Maybe he thinks she cannot control her horse. Maybe he is correct? For a moment Ria wonders the same thing. Yet with tightened reins, leaning back and with a quick voice command to whoa, Tonka, like the champion he is, starts to slow. Ears flickering as he registers her words, he slows to a canter, then a trot and then reluctantly, his opinions signalled by a snort, to a walk. His continued reluctance demonstrated by the odd prance, thrown in every few steps or so, as if to check whether Ria can be convinced to see reason and be persuaded to change her mind. She leans forward, carefully, so as not to encourage him, and pats him on the neck.

'No Tonka, you old devil. That is more than enough for my poor, sore behind!'

The newly learnt ritual then follows - of unsaddling, washing down and turning out Tonka into his paddock. Ria now familiar with this routine needs no help from Ben. Once Tonka is finally ensconced in his paddock, Ria then turns and looks for Ben. She finds him in the stable yard with Trixie. Trixie, so heavy in foal, leans against Ben as he scratches under her chin.

'Not long to go old girl, hey?'

He turns to Ria.

'It could be tonight. Certainly, in the next day or so. See, her milk is coming in – so she must be very close. We should check her before bed tonight. Although if she is like most mares I know, she would prefer to have her baby when we aren't looking. Maybe it's a girl thing?'

He turns to Ria.

'Fancy going to the pub tonight? To celebrate surviving your first week here? A few of my mates will be there – not sure who exactly, but maybe Geordie,' he concludes with a slight smirk.

Was she really that obvious?

Trying not to display any inappropriate eagerness, Ria tilts her head as she considers this invitation and then indicates her consent.

'Provided Aunt Kat is OK with that?'

'Oh, she won't miss us in the slightest. Mum likes a bit of solitude and will enjoy a night to herself.'

Ria, not convinced about this, checks with her aunt when she returns to the house. Ria's protestations are dismissed with a laugh

'Of course. You go out with Ben. You young ones need a bit of excitement – such as it is out here in the sticks. Go on. Otherwise you will be stuck out here on the farm without a break, and that will drive you senseless with boredom.'

That evening Ria finds herself once again in the old farm utility heading up the now familiar dirt road into *town* – or more accurately the small village known as *Kings Vale*.

Dressed in newish clean jeans, topped with a sparkly top and leather jacket, she just hopes she isn't overdressed for a night out at the local pub. Even Ben, she notices, has made an effort. The fly away hair is freshly washed and tied back into a ponytail. His scruffy beard is no longer, having been shaved away, revealing a strong jawline and a dimple that makes a fleeting appearance when he smiles at her. He really is rather gorgeous, she thinks, taking in this new improved Ben with a sideways glance.

The pub is located in the main street, just down from the railway station and was the building Ria saw in the distance only a week ago, when she was waiting for her unpunctual cousin. A week ago, she could see a few cars parked outside. Tonight, the street resembles a car park packed with a variety of farm vehicles, some new, some dinted and damaged, but all dirty and dusty. Some with dogs tied in the back, clearly familiar with the routine judging by the way they are sprawled at ease waiting for their master – or mistress.

A crush of people out on the front footpath – all with a beverage in hand and all in full flow of conversation. Ben's arrival is greeted with increased noise – cheers, yells and catcalls. A cacophony of noise – very little of it understandable, but out of the mayhem Ria can discern cries of – 'At last Ben.' 'Who's your lady?' 'It's your shout you slacker.' And then a voice she recognises and an arm waving above the crowd.

'Over here Ben and Ria. This way!'

Ben grabs her by the arm and they head in the direction of the waving arm. It is Geordie – standing by the outside wall of the pub, with a few of the people Ria recognises from the open garden event. They all greet her like a long-lost friend and quickly settle into conversation, wanting to know what she has been doing and checking that Ben has been taking good care of her.

The laughter of new-found friends, the sharing of anecdotes and re-enactment of dramas, all enhanced with liquid refreshments and then simple pub food as the evening progresses relaxes Ria.

Her pleasure enhanced by Ben's warm affection and by Geordie's glances of interest. Without conscious thought, she finds herself smiling and laughing along with the others. Her memories of sorrow easing and washing away with each laugh – or giggle.

On the drive home Ben comments:

'I think you have an admirer.'

'Me?'

'Yeah, Geordie. I've never seen him so animated and I don't think it was the drink doing it. He's quite shy you know. A bit like me!'

She can sense his smile and, in the darkness, glimpses a glimmer of teeth.

To this she gives a bit of a snort – a ladylike one at that – to indicate a degree of disbelief. All the while thinking that any interest from Geordie would not be altogether unwelcome. For to her mind, his attractions are becoming more and more apparent the more she gets to know him. Of course, she has only seen him twice, but there is something about Geordie – the twinkle in his eyes, his smiling good humour or even something as elemental as his masculine scent that intrigues her. His close friendship with Ben speaks of a kind and caring person. Then tonight as they left, Geordie took her by the hand – her dainty hand enveloped by his enormous paw – and immediately his touch sent shivers through her. In that instant, when he released her hand, she felt a profound sense of loss as if part of her had just been cut loose. This feeling of being incomplete and lacking a part of her being was so new to her and felt with such intensity, that all she wanted to do was to snatch his hand back again.

Ben's voice intrudes on her thoughts.

'He does you know. I bet we'll see him again – maybe even tomorrow. Take your cousin Ben's advice. I know so much about relationships – not!' He laughs, 'But Geordie is a good one, a keeper – don't let him go.'

He swerves suddenly and with a muttered 'shit' steers the car to avoid a kangaroo crossing the road. Ria notices that they are now back on the dirt road, climbing up the hill. The trees that line each side of the road loom around them with menace and evidently provide shelter for wildlife, such as the now vanishing kangaroo. Ben swerves to avoid several more, all the while muttering under his breath about the idiocy of such animals. Ria, glancing around can see clusters of small kangaroos lit by the car lights as they pass, all focussed on grazing the new growth by the side of the road.

'That recent rain – you know - the other week,' Ben explains. 'A bit of growth from the rain and it brings them all out. Can't blame them. They're hungry. The young ones have no road sense – yet to learn to avoid cars. Well, either they will, or they'll be dead meat.'

Having crested the hill, they follow the road down into the valley and across the clatter of the wooden bridge. Turning left through the farm gates Ben heads away from the house to the stables. To Ria's concerned glance he explains:

'Just a quick detour – the old girl you know. I want to check that she is ok. When we saw her this morning I had my suspicions.'

He stops the car out behind the stables. Taking a torch out of the glovebox they step out into the warmth of the calm evening and head towards Trixie's stall. Ben slows, his finger at his lips to indicate they should remain silent. Carefully, so as not to disturb the mare, he shines his torch towards but not directly into the stable. In the low light it is clear Trixie's time has come.

By the dim light Ria can see that the mare is lying on her side in the straw. Apart from a flicker of an ear, Trixie doesn't register their presence. Her entire being is focussed on what is happening to her body. Ben with finger on lips, places the torch on the ledge by the stable door and whispers:

'I'll just go back and turn on the outside light. That'll give us enough light to see by. Please be as quiet as you can. It is critical we don't frighten the old girl. Any sudden noise or strong light could cause her to scare and damage herself. But we can stay here and make sure she gets through this ok.'

Outside light now turned on Ben returns. The indirect light is sufficient for them to see the effort the mare exerts with each contraction.

'Not long now,' says Ben as he points to the dainty hoof appearing and then receding with each contraction. A strong contraction and with a massive grunt one leg quickly followed by another appears. And then the shape of a head covered by a milky sheet, a bit like a plastic bag.

'Oh, oh,' whispers Ben. 'The membrane hasn't ruptured. We need to help out or the foal will suffocate. Quietly now – just ease into the stall. If you sit by her head and keep Trixie calm I will do what I can to help the foal. No sudden movements though.'

Now Ria has delivered many babies, but this is the first time she has helped deliver a foal. Yet the fundamental principle is the same – keep calm and help the mother – be it human or animal. In soft undertones, she murmurs to the straining mare, telling her what a champion she is, all the while keeping an eye on Ben, who gently eases the membrane away from the foal's face. With one more massive contraction the foal slithers out and draws its first breath. Ben signals to Ria that they can move back, which they do, sliding backwards towards the stable door, where they sit and watch. Mare and foal lie still, seemingly overcome with the exhaustion of it all. In response to Ria's anxious look Ben smiles and whispers:

'It's all ok. They both need to rest and Trixie needs to deliver the placenta. That may take a little while – maybe another twenty minutes or so.'

Sure enough he is right. After some time, during which humans and animals all sit or lie quietly, the placenta is delivered in a rush.

'I'll need to grab the placenta in a minute so the vet can check it tomorrow, but no rush. Let's just enjoy the moment.'

As if on command Trixie and her baby both stir and start the effort of standing up. Ria notices Ben looking anxious and asks why.

'I just want to be sure nothing goes wrong. This is the time when a mare cannot get to her feet straight away and in her struggle could stand on her foal. I've seen foal's legs broken that way and believe me that is something to be avoided!'

But with an enormous grunt Trixie is on her feet and then nuzzling her baby to do likewise. With shaky legs, the foal struggles to its feet and leans onto mum.

'Pretty special – eh?' says Ben, smiling excitedly at Ria. 'Though I guess you've seen lots of deliveries of the human kind with your career and all that?'

'A fair few – and of course, each one is special. Oh, but this one - well it's my first foal and it is equally wondrous. Oh look! It's noticed us!'

'She – not it. Do you mind! A bit of respect please. And let her look at you. Once she is standing we can get a bit closer and say hello. We need to let our scent and voice imprint on her memory.'

Turning to Trixie, who is gently nuzzling her baby, Ben murmurs, 'Well done old girl. She's a beauty – just like you.'

The silence of the still evening wraps around them as they are caught up in the wonder that is a new life. Ben, eyes sparkling, speaks of how this little foal, so like Trixie's others, is perhaps even better and then expands on his plans for her. No intention to let her go. Being the last of Trixie's foals she is precious. No more babies for Trixie. She is too old for that and will be free to live out the rest of her life at leisure, as the matron of the herd. Perhaps, Ben suggests, she might even be a calming influence on the others.

Sometime later and with her mother's encouraging, by way of a gentle nudge, the foal still standing on wobbly legs, starts to move in teetering steps. Driven by instinct she muzzles at her mother's flank, until she eventually locates her mother's teats and starts hungrily sucking like a born natural.

Trixie stands still, apart from an occasional sniff at her baby, as if to check that all is well. She does not object to her baby's sucking. Ben, watching carefully explains that it is not always that straightforward. Sometimes, even the most experienced mother will reject a newborn foal. Some of them never have the mothering instinct, and that is when a bit of assistance is needed.

'Not the case here, though. I can see we will have no problems with Trixie tonight. I'll just go and mix up a bit of feed for her and then I think we can safely leave them for the rest of the night.'

With that Ben leaves Ria and wanders off to the feed room. In the silence, broken only by the slurping sound of sucking, Ria relaxes and leans against the wall, taking in the sights, smells, and sounds around her. The lingering earthy smell of the afterbirth and wet new life mingles with Trixie's horsey aroma, the scent of hay, manure and pasture all blend to create aromas a city girl like Ria has never before experienced. Yet these smells are not objectionable. To her mind, much more preferable than those generated by exhaust, asphalt, and fast-food outlets. She breathes in deeply and sends a brief message of gratitude to the universe.

A new life, a fresh miracle, and a message from the universe that even after sorrow, life goes on in all its wonder.

Chapter Ten

The next morning Ria awakens slowly and ponders why she feels so tired. It almost feels like she has experienced a dream. The delivery of a new life into that dark and silent world now makes her question if it really happened, or whether it was her imagination at play.

Yet when she sees Ben at the breakfast table full of excitement and telling his mother about the previous night's adventures, she realises that it really did happen.

'I couldn't have done it without Ria there to sit by Trixie and keep her calm. For a little while there it was a bit touch and go, and I really needed an extra set of hands. Thank goodness we stopped to check on Trixie on the way home or the outcome might have been so much worse.'

After wiping his mouth with the serviette Ben pushes himself away from the table.

'That's it for me. Must go check on the old girl and wait for the vet. He should be here shortly to see how Trixie and the foal are, and also to look over the placenta to check if all of it has been delivered. Ria what are your plans? Want to join me?'

Ria looks at her aunt who smiles back.

'No. If it is ok with you, I'll help Aunt Kat tidy up and then maybe lend a hand if she wants. I've seen enough placentas in my time. No wish to see any more!'

The rest of the morning passes smoothly. It's now a week to the next function and Ria finds herself tasked with a range of tidying-up chores – from polishing furniture in the formal reception rooms to weeding and watering the flower beds that line the courtyard. Not tasks she would normally look forward to doing, but somehow in the company of her aunt they become strangely pleasurable. With each item polished her aunt explains its history, and that somehow detracts from the tedium of the activity.

'So much of the furniture in these rooms belonged to my husband's ancestors. I sometimes feel like I live in a museum peopled by the remnants of other people's lives – not my own,' her aunt explains, 'especially in this, the formal sitting room. Not much has changed for generations – except for the addition of electricity and even that is sometimes a bit hit and miss! But our customers like the way this room is furnished, so I suppose I shouldn't complain. Nowadays these rooms only get used for functions. The kitchen and family room do me just fine.'

Together they stand, shoulder to shoulder and observe the symmetry and beauty of the room. In Ria's opinion, it is a rather gracious and welcoming room. Wide polished honey-coloured floorboards, high ceilings with moulded cornice work and an ornate moulded plaster ceiling rose catch her eye. Through the windows she can see the garden framed by the last of the autumn roses. At one end of the room a marble fireplace flanked by glass fronted cedar bookcases, crammed with books crying out to be read. At the other end of the room half open folding doors beckon, a glimpse of the old ballroom just visible through the opening. It doesn't take much for Ria to visualise these rooms in days long past, filled with laughter and music. Maybe that is how it will be at the weekend when the function is in full swing?

Outside in the courtyard warmed by the autumn sunshine Ria weeds, while her aunt dead heads the roses. At one point her aunt, with one warning hand on her arm, alerts her to stillness. As she looks at her aunt in alarm, her aunt by tilt of head directs her attention towards the courtyard path leading to the cottages. There crossing the path, a sinuous brown snake, paying them no mind and intent on its own journey.

'See I told you,' her aunt whispers. 'Stand still, until it has moved on and we will all be fine. It's really quite simple. Keep out of their way and they will keep out of ours.'

Ria struggles to repress the instinctive feelings of revulsion and the shudders she can feel moving down her spine. Yet, as she gazes at the creature gliding along the path intent on its own passage, she grudgingly acknowledges to herself the shimmery beauty of the animal. The gloss of the scales and the muscular ripples of its body as it moves in a rhythmic manner are something to be marvelled at, even as her very being urges her to flee.

'Aunt Kat I don't know how you can be so calm,' she whispers, watching the tail end of the snake disappear with a flicker under a bush on the side of the path. 'I'm not sure I can ever get used to sharing my home with those – those creatures.'

'You'd be surprised what you can get used to. It only takes a bit of common sense – you know like using a torch at night. Keeping an eye out and understanding the sort of places where they will be – well it will then be surprising if you see too many. They do tend to keep out of our way and if you see one - just stand still. Oh, and of course try not to tread on one! For some reason snakes don't like that!'

That night Ria recounts her day's adventures over the phone to Penny who, to Ria's bemusement, finds it all unaccountably funny.

'Yeah, you can laugh from the safety of your inner-city refuge. It's alright for you. It's a wonder my hair didn't turn white – I was so terrified!'

'You seem to have forgotten about the redback spiders out the back here, and it is only a matter of time until one of those funnel web spiders turns up in our garden. It's a jungle everywhere. Lucky, you studied nursing. And speaking of your nursing, how is your baby? The foal?'

'She's just gorgeous. All leggy and frisky. I plan to go and see her every day and I want to spend time with her, brushing and patting her. Ben says the more time we spend with her now, the better it will be for later on. He's teaching me how to best handle her. He showed me today how he teaches her to lead – just with his arms and not with any halter or lead rope. It's amazing. He puts one arm around her neck and with a bit of pressure by using the other arm around her bum, encourages her forward. And 'cause we have been patting and rubbing her since birth, she is so relaxed when we touch her face or neck. She just loves a scratch – as does her mum. Her mum is getting a bit of attention too.'

'Has your baby a name?'

'Mmmm. I think she is going to be called Starry. She has a perfect white star in the middle of her forehead.'

'What a lovely name. And it sounds like you're having fun. I'll never get you back here! And by the way thank you for sending Shelley to stay. She's heading back to you tomorrow, but I'm going to miss her. What a sweet girl. I am so tempted to ask her to stay.'

'Don't you dare Penny! You promised to behave. What would Aunt Kat say?'

'Well, she'll be moving on shortly. Shelley tells me she has plans to head to Queensland. It's only a matter of time – just make sure you come home. I miss you dear.'

And with that, Ria realises she misses her not quite aunt and the familiarity of home. With mutual exchange of assurances of love and affection the call ends. For a moment Ria sits by the phone pondering what to do. Her aunt has been giving every indication that she would like her to stay for an indefinite period and, with Shelley possibly leaving soon, she can understand why her aunt might want some extra help. In many ways, the thought of staying on the farm for a longer period is rather appealing. Spending time with Ben is well – fun. He is so positive, chirpy and full of enthusiasm – a bit like a scruffy family pet – a Labrador maybe? – that it's hard not to be swept along with excitement for whatever task or activity he is involving her in. Sure, there are times his face clouds over and she becomes aware of the sorrow that lurks just under the surface, or those occasions when she senses his frustration as once again, the farm chores drag him away from his sculpting. Yet the disturbance brought about is momentary, a bit like a cloud passing over the sun and with a disciplined shake of his head she sees him push the sorrow or frustration to one side, as he forces himself to focus on the present and the task at hand.

So much to enjoy. Every day Ria wakes with enthusiasm – looking forward to time spent outdoors with the horses and with a certain foal. Even the help her aunt needs in the garden is enjoyed. After so many years spent indoors in the sterile hospital environment, with its all-pervading smell of antiseptic and the other unpleasant smells associated with nursing, being outside is a newfound treat. The chill of the morning air warming as the autumn day progresses and the simple pleasure of turning her face to feel the sun, reminds her of how many simple pleasures she has missed in recent times, as she juggled work with the needs of her mother.

Yes, leaving here would not be easy. Yet sooner or later she must – there is only so much leave from work that she can take and at some stage she must return, back to Penny and back to that house at Glebe, that echoes with the sounds and memories of a life shared with her mother. But can she return with so many questions unanswered and more and more mysteries to solve? Why did her mother leave? Why did her uncle kill himself and what happened to Kitty?

Chapter Eleven

The Saturday of the wedding function dawns in a mass of red and orange.

'I don't like the look of today,' says her aunt over breakfast. 'You saw the red sunrise – red in the morning, shepherd's warning and all that. I checked the weather report. We could be in for showers late afternoon. Let's hope they've got it wrong. Wet weddings can be a bit tricky.'

Shelley, who had returned the day before full of tales about the big city, tries to sound positive.

'Well, we should be fine. The marquee just off the courtyard is up and looks almost ready to go. And the caterers are finishing putting up the tables now. That leaves the tablecloths to be done and the cutlery and then the flowers can go on the tables. If it does rain we will be fine. We may have to hand out umbrellas to get them from the ceremony in the sitting room to the marquee. It'll all be grand Kat. We've done this so many times before – it should run like clockwork.'

'I hope you are right Shelley. Better it runs like clockwork in fine weather though. Come on you two, we still have a bit to do. I'll organise the florist and the caterer. Shelley please do a last run through the rooms and the loos. Check everything is perfect – oh and make sure the signs for parking are up. And Ria – it's as I promised – the leaf blower for you! Just do the best you can.'

By noon both house and marquee look like something out of a classy wedding magazine. Swags of white netting drape the inside of the marquee. Autumnal fruits, rose hips and flowers decorate the middle of each table and a forest of trees line the walls. In the sitting room, a floral archway has been installed around the doorway leading to the ballroom, from where the bridal party will appear. Rows of chairs are arrayed in the sitting room for the guests, all chairs facing the marble fireplace, in front of which a small hall table has been placed, covered with fine linen and on which another floral arrangement has been displayed.

The bride is now ensconced in the spare guest cottage by the creek – ostensibly to finalise her preparations with the support of her mother and the bridesmaids – but judging from the number of bottles of champagne they were all seen to be carrying as they headed that way – they possibly had other ideas in mind.

The groom and friends have sometime earlier been escorted into one of the spare bedrooms, again for the purpose of getting ready, but judging from the popping sounds of beer cans opening and the increasing hilarity, *getting ready* may actually be a very inaccurate description of what is actually occurring.

Ria, dressed like her aunt and Shelley in black shirt and trousers, hovers by her aunt waiting for further instructions.

'I think we have time for a bit of a relax. Maybe a quick cup of tea. Although we should keep an eye and an ear out for the guests. Ben is in the garden somewhere on traffic duty, but we do need to be by the front door to welcome our guests and direct them inside.

Mugs of tea in hand all three find a spot in the corner of the kitchen to sit and observe the organised chaos of the caterers. For some hours now, they have been in charge of the kitchen, finalising the food for the wedding feast. Much of the food has been prepared off site and brought over in large plastic tubs, but there is still chopping, tossing and decorating. Earlier Ria had caught a glimpse of an impressive croquembouche wedding cake being carried under careful supervision out to the marquee. Now the caterers are focussed on arranging trays of hors d'oeuvres to be consumed with the pre-dinner drinks once the ceremony is finished. Ria's tummy rumbles as she contemplates the delicious food being laid out before her.

Aunt Kat notices and laughs.

'Enough of that child. If you're lucky there might be some leftovers for us later. But for now we'd better get cracking. Come on, finish your tea. I can hear people. We need to get outside.'

By the time they get to the front door they find people already arriving, laughing and chattering, bearing presents and dressed in their finery for the occasion. Ria directs them to a room off the entry, where the presents can be left, and then hands them over to her aunt and Shelley, who take turns in escorting people into the sitting room.

So many people of so many ages, but a lot already known to each other judging by the amount of laughter and conversation that fills the room. Infants cry and children squeal as their parents try to restrain them, with little success.

Her aunt comes near.

'I'm not sure how much longer this mob will remain calm. I think we have most of the guests here. There are not too many spare seats left. Shelley, would you please go and round up the groom and his attendants and I'll run down and see how the bride is getting on. The celebrant is starting to look a bit stressed. Would you please deal with her Ria? See if you can settle her down.'

They gaze at the celebrant who, out the front of the now crowded room, is pacing up and down reading her notes and visibly muttering to herself.

'Yes, you go. I think it might help the celebrant if I can take her away from all the noise. Don't want her scaring the crowd! She can stand with me out in the entrance until the groom appears and they can then go in together.'

For what feels like ages to Ria, she and the celebrant stand together and make small talk. The celebrant, an anxious middle-aged woman confidingly tells Ria that this is only her second ceremony. The first one ended in disaster when the bride fainted at the altar and the groom got cold feet just before saying his vows. Altogether not an auspicious start to what she hopes will be a lucrative career. But so much can go wrong and, as the celebrant outlines a catalogue of disasters that she assures Ria have been endured by her fellow celebrants, Ria starts to appreciate why the celebrant is anxious. Ria had never realised what a risky business a marriage ceremony could be.

They hear the groom's party before they come into sight. Striding, or maybe it would be better described as stumbling, up the enclosed veranda from the bedroom. The sound of their singing precedes them. Could those be rugby tunes that they are singing? Involving women of loose virtue? Surely not the stuff for weddings? With a quick *excuse me* to the celebrant, Ria darts up the veranda towards the approaching party.

'Excellent, here you are. Come this way. The celebrant wants a quick chat before you take your places. Here give me that,' she says grabbing a half empty can of beer from the groom before he can object. 'I'll hold onto it until after the ceremony.'

She pushes the groom towards the celebrant, waits for a moment until she is certain that the celebrant is in control, then heads out the front door towards the cottage to look for her aunt.

Inside the cottage she finds a scene of chaos. The bride in tears, with her mother trying to calm her down. Aunt Kat in close conversation with one of the bridesmaids looks concerned. She looks up as Ria enters and grimaces.

'There you are dear. A slight problem...'

'No, not slight. A disaster,' wails the bride to be. 'My top. It won't do up. See it's too tight around the bust. It fit two weeks ago at the last fitting, but now I can't get it to close. What am I to do? That dressmaker has made a complete mess,' she shrieks and then breaks into hysterical sobs.

It is clear that there is a problem as the bride turns to show the gaping back in the under bodice that obviously has not the capacity to do up. The lace overlay lies discarded on the bed.

Maybe it is Ria's entrance into this chaos as a new player to the drama or maybe it is her calm manner, but all now look to her for a solution. The bride's tears subside into soft hiccoughing sobs. Ria enters the room and comes alongside the bride.

'Hi there. Carla, isn't it? I'm Ria, Aunty Kat's niece. Let me have a look and we'll see if there is a solution. Yes, I see what you mean. It really is a bit too small isn't it around the bust. I suppose we could try strapping you to make your bust smaller, but I think that might show. Let me think. You have the lace overlay, which I'm assuming is not so fitted?'

The bride nods in reply.

'Alright then. I suppose we need to think of something else to go on underneath. You're not on the catwalks of Paris, so I guess you wouldn't want to aim for the see-through look...'

'Mind you,' interjects one of the bridesmaids, a sister judging from her likeness to the bride, 'that might be worth doing just to see the faces of our old biddy aunts – and Uncle Humphrey would probably have an apoplexy!'

'Frances this is not the time,' scolds the mother. But all the others, including the bride, laugh and somehow the atmosphere of doom lightens.

'Ok, so that might be a possibility of last resort. However, I have another suggestion. That is if you don't mind wearing something I have on?'

Ria starts to unbutton her very staid black shirt to reveal a strappy, ivory coloured camisole – its sweetheart neckline is embroidered with delicate flowers in the same ivory tone.

'It's my favourite, you see, and I often wear it to feel a little bit fancy – especially when I am in my boring black shirt – sorry Aunty Kat, but you must admit it is a boring shirt.'

Aunty Kat nods and smiles. The bride draws nearer, her hand reaching out to inspect the item of clothing under consideration. Comprehension dawns.

'You mean you would lend it to me to wear now?'

'Sure, no problem so long as you don't mind wearing something I have been wearing. Though I did have a shower this morning and it is clean. It's stretchy and should fit around your bust. I think it'll look fine under the lace. Come on let's give it a go.'

With that Ria whips off the camisole and hands it to Carla, who in turns puts it on. It fits. The lace overlay is now put on, the billowing tulle skirt stepped into and done up and a bridal vision now appears – albeit with rather smudged makeup, where the mascara has run from the bridal tears.

'There, perfect. It looks like you always intended to wear that undergarment,' says her mother. 'Now let's just adjust that makeup, put on your veil and you are ready to go. Can't keep the groom waiting for you now. He'll be getting anxious.'

Or he might just have had enough time to sober up, thinks Ria, not so charitably.

She leaves the bridal party, who are now in a focussed flap, and heads back to the house. Standing outside the front door is Ben, who greets her arrival with some anxiety.

'At last. What's going on? The groom is looking worried and the troops are restless, especially the little ones. They're all a fidget.'

'Not long to go now. There was a bit of a wardrobe malfunction. All fixed now. Just some last-minute adjustments. Let's go and tell the celebrant and the groom.'

Arm in arm they wander into the front foyer where the groom and the celebrant are huddled. They look up as the door opens, clearly anticipating a different couple entering the room. When it is clear it is not the bride and her father, they both rush across and bombard Ria with questions.

'Where is she?' demands the groom.

'Is there a problem?' asks the celebrant at the same time, so their words overlay, and it takes a moment for Ria to disentangle them.

'It's ok. Just a slight costume glitch. All sorted, and she will be here any minute.'

Now looking at the groom, Ria continues: 'Shouldn't you be up at the altar – or what we are using as an altar?'

He nods and moves off into the main room, where his mates are waiting. The chatter in the room hushes and all look towards the floral arch at the back of the room in anticipation. Music swells and as if by magic a bridal vision of loveliness appears, arm in arm with her beaming father and preceded by the now serene bridesmaids. Ria and Ben withdraw to the entry foyer and content themselves with a quick peek through the now ajar door.

'She's lovely. It's as if all that commotion and drama never happened. Like this is all proceeding exactly as planned.'

'What happened?'

'Come outside and I'll tell you. We aren't needed here.'

They stand outside on the gravelled driveway and as Ria recounts in full, albeit with some slight exaggeration, the drama that she had just witnessed, she notices that Ben is not paying her his full attention. His reaction to when she outlines the possibility of a bride in a see-through top is so underwhelming that she pauses, and then asks:

'OK. Out with it. You're not really listening. What's bothering you?'

'I'm listening. I am. It's just …well, look around you. See.' And with that he points towards the southern horizon where an ominous grey sky is developing, roiling, massing black clouds piling one on top of another in the distance, and slowly creeping forward.

'I noticed the sky a little while back and checked the weather forecast. We're in for some bad weather this afternoon. Rain, wind and so on. I only hope it misses us, but I don't like our chances'.

'Surely nothing else can go wrong? Surely?'

'Don't you believe it. This place is just a magnet for disaster!'

As if to prove Ria correct and Ben wrong, the wedding ceremony proceeds as planned. The emotional ceremony over, the joyful couple and relieved guests spill out onto the courtyard, where they quickly devour the canapes and gulp beverages. Small children freed from the binds of best behaviour, whoop and call as they play complicated games of chasings around the veranda and through the throng. Yet the crowd are so focussed on their socialising, that the children and their antics are happily ignored.

The dinner in the marquee goes without a hitch. Although the caterers are fully in control of the process of feeding the crowd, Ria and Ben are kept busy in a support role to both guests and caterers – escorting guests to the bathroom, retrieving lost shawls or children and locating extra items for the caterers. Aunt Kat and Shelley meanwhile are in the kitchen supervising the activities there and dealing with any last-minute dramas, which Aunt Kat has already assured her always happen.

It's not until the speeches are underway that Ria, standing beside Ben at the doorway of the marquee, notices the way the shrubs in the courtyard are rustling and looks at Ben with concern.

'Yep. I think we're in for it. This is the start of the storm. There are umbrellas in that tub on the veranda if we need them, but hopefully we'll be fine.'

The wind as if to contradict him, swells and howls as it passes the courtyard entrance. Eddies gust inwards and swirl the leaves now being shaken from the massive tree in the courtyard centre. In the distance Ria can hear the not so sheltering trees in the garden as they are shaken and tossed by the storm. Not that far away an ominous crack and then a crash as some tree limb falls to the ground. The lights flicker and dim.

'Well, that does it,' says Ben. 'Looks like we've lost power. Lucky those lights on the tables are battery powered, but we will need to locate some more torches. Here, take these two and I'll go and find some more. I'll just check with the caterers to see if they are ok, or if they want me to bring up the generator. Keep away from that big tree, won't you?'

He disappears into the now dark house heading for the kitchen, leaving an increasingly worried Ria standing at the marquee entrance.

With the loss of power impacting on the effectiveness of the sound system, all speeches grind to a halt. The MC shouting at the top of his voice assures everyone all is fine and that given the next speech was to be delivered by the groom, it's just as well they're missing it. He urges everyone to relax and enjoy the wine, and that dessert will be distributed shortly. The howling wind drowns out his words. People towards the back of the marquee do not hear what he is saying. They lean forward, as if asking one another what is happening. Children run to their parents and climb onto laps, also leaning in, as if to seek comfort.

Meanwhile the wind howls around the marquee, screeching and yowling like so many demented cats. A sudden gust and with a loud snap a supporting rope breaks free. The now loosened far side of the marquee starts to flap with increasing viciousness. People rise from their chairs and look around, uncertain as to what to do, but instinctively knowing they must do something. A further snap and more of the marquee breaks free from its restraints

Keeping her voice calm, but in full shout, Ria speaks up. Those close to her can hear, but those further way struggle forward as soon as they notice she is speaking.

'Everyone. Listen up please. I suggest we move back into the formal sitting rooms, where we will be out of this wind. If you would all head this way, and then we will be able to relax into dessert away from the storm. This way please.'

She directs those near to her, then moves to the bridal table. The bride has reverted to her earlier tears. Ria crouches down by her side.

'It's ok. We'll get everyone inside and then we can continue with the party. My cousin has gone to get the generator. If the caterers don't need it, we will set it up nearby, so you can have lights and music. Come on. Let's get you inside.'

'But my cake,' the bride wails.' We haven't cut the cake and look - the tent is collapsing!'

Ria looks across over the remaining people, now moving through and out of the marquee. Sure enough, one side of the marquee's roof is sagging, as well as two walls flapping in the wind. It is only a matter of time until the entire marquee collapses in on itself. And there in the middle of the marquee, resplendent on a small circular table, the wedding cake. And not just any wedding cake, but a towering croquembouche, glistening with golden toffee and surrounded by a garland of flowers.

Ria gulps. How to move that? Well, it was moved into place there, so it must be possible.

'I'll take care of that,' she says. 'Get yourself inside, and you two' – pointing at the groomsmen – 'come and give me a hand.'

The bridal couple scarper hand in hand, as Ria and her two companions, rugby players by the muscle-bound look of them, move to the cake and try to determine how to move it.

'If you two would lift and carry the table, I could walk beside and try to keep that thing from falling over. But we need to move now– we don't have much time.'

Who knew a simple croquembouche would be so heavy or so cumbersome? *What was wrong with the wedding cake of choice for generations – a fruit cake and none of this fancy stuff?* Ria thinks as they struggle to move out the marquee and up the veranda steps. With every step, the towering mass wobbles and threatens to collapse. Ria finds herself using both arms to balance the structure. The wind teases and whips the surrounding flowers away and does its best to push the croquembouche over, as Ria summons all her reserves to fight back. They make it up the steps with tower intact – just - cake and carriers all dampened by the wind driven rain. The cake manoeuvred through opened doors and into the formal lounge room, where cake and its carriers are greeted by a cheering crowd.

'It got a bit damp,' Ria confides to the hovering bride, as she supervises the boys settling cake and table in place. 'Probably best if you cut it now and share it out before the toffee dissolves completely.'

'Thank you so much,' the bride gushes. 'I don't know what I would have done if the cake hadn't been saved.'

'Had hysterics probably,' one of the boys mutters, as he moves away. Fortunately, not overheard by the bride, as she continues to gush:

'You've now saved the day – twice. I cannot thank you enough,' all this said as the bride tries to embrace Ria. Ria gently disengages the brides' hands and moves away.

'Best if you don't get too close. I'm covered in toffee – not a good look for a bride if you get this toffee on you. But when you cut the cake I wouldn't mind a piece. It looks SO delicious.'

The cake cut, the final speeches made and all settle into clusters of groups around the room on the rearranged chairs from the wedding ceremony. By this time Ben has returned with the generator which, installed in the courtyard and with leads running into the formal lounge, is powering several lamps. The room lit by these lamps and with a scattering of battery-operated candles retrieved from the now defunct marquee, looks darkly atmospheric and mysterious. Or romantic, according to one of the guests. A battery-operated radio located by Ben and tuned to *non-stop party hits* is in place in the old ball room – also lit by those battery-operated candles. In that room, the children and younger guests dance wildly to tunes that were popular in the eighties – long before many of these dancers were born.

The storm continues until the wee small hours and is blowing itself out at about the same time as the wedding guests. The older guests leave first – after expressing amazement at how late it is and how long they lasted.

One such guest speculates: 'maybe it was because we could relax in the lounge room?'

'What a cool party', says another younger guest, whilst being dragged out the front door by exhausted parents.

The bride and groom still linger – slow dancing on the dance floor to some long-forgotten eighties tune. Ben draws near and taps the groom on the shoulder.

'Here mate, do you want this torch to light your way to the cottage or will I walk you down?'

Offer of an escort duly accepted, Ben and the happy couple disappear, leaving Ria and her aunt to wave farewell to the last of the guests.

'I don't think the creek will be flooded yet,' says her aunt. 'But I suppose we will know for sure if they all return because they can't get across! But I think it should be ok. The storm was largely wind and fury – the rain being blown around with such ferociousness that it seemed much more than it actually was. Come on let's go get a cuppa and then bed. The caterers have done a lot of the tidying, but they will return in the morning to do the rest.'

Sitting by the still warm Aga, drinking hot tea from mugs decorated with dogs and horses, they are both silent until her aunt gives a huge sigh.

'Well, I've never seen a wedding quite like that one. Nearly everything that could go wrong went wrong. All we need now is for the bridal cottage to leak – or there to be a possum in the roof! That would be the icing on the cake!'

'Don't even mention it aunt. I think we all did amazingly well – all things considered. A bride who looked so lovely despite her wardrobe malfunction and didn't have to resort to giving the elderly relatives apoplexy with a see-through top. A sort of sober groom. A great feed and we saved the cake! Pity about the marquee – but I suppose the damage can be assessed in the morning? Maybe it won't be completely destroyed?'

'Mmmm. Maybe. But not our problem,' says her aunt as she takes a thoughtful sip of her tea.

Ben coming through the side door, shaking raindrops from his curls, hears the last few words and asks:

'What problem?'

'Nothing dear – just talking about the marquee.'

He draws up a chair and, looking thoughtful, turns to his mother. His hand on hers, he looks at his mother, his eyes serious – or as much of them as Ria can see from under his wet, shaggy fringe.

'Ma. Now listen up. I've just had a call from Kitty and….'

'Kitty?' Ria's aunt says in a shaky voice.

'Yeah. Please just listen – wait 'til I've said my bit, then you can ask questions.'

Ria's aunt nods.

'Kitty's rung me from Sydney. Says she wants to come home. Not sure if this is for a visit or for longer – but I guess we'll find out when we see her. Anyway, she wants me to drive up to Sydney and bring her back here. I said I'd go first thing in the morning. That way we'll be home late afternoon. Now mum, don't get your hopes up. We don't know what she has been doing or taking while she's been away. She could be very different to the Kitty we once knew. And she doesn't know about dad. I'll tell her that on the way back.'

Ben pauses, takes a close look at his mother and clearly is concerned by what he sees as he continues:

'Are you ok?'

His mother is obviously not ok. Tears form and well in her eyes. Any words she is trying to say are obscured by the shuddering sobs that convulse her body. Ben reaches across and wraps his mum in his strong, damp arms. He holds her close, murmuring words of comfort in the soft tones Ria has only recently heard him use with the foal. Like the foal, Ria's aunt also quietens and soon rests quietly in her son's arms.

'I'm ok,' she says. 'It's the shock you know. I never thought I'd see my daughter again. I suppose this should be a joyous occasion, but we have to tell her about her father – and I'm dreading how she will take it.'

Turning to Ria, her aunt continues:

'You see she was always so close to her father. I'm sure you don't mind me saying it Ben, but she clearly was his favourite – his little princess.'

'Yeah mum. I know. And to be honest I don't mind anymore. I might have once, but being his favourite came at a cost. He had such high expectations of Kitty – so much pressure on her to excel and I managed to miss out on that. He was pretty tough on her. Nothing she did was good enough, and she tried so hard.'

'She did, didn't she?' His mum agrees. 'Yes, he was tough on Kitty, but she adored him. Even from when she was little she was his little shadow. Always with him whatever farm chores he was doing – whether on her pony or with him in the old farm truck – they were a team. Then something went wrong when she was about 16, and she would have nothing to do with him. That's when she became answerable to no-one – wild and rebellious. I just hope she has changed now she is a bit older.'

'Maybe, but I guess we'll know for sure when we see her tomorrow,' says Ben, pushing his chair back. 'Come on you two. It's been a long day and we all need our rest.'

Chapter Twelve

Ben is long gone by the time Ria and Shelley wander up to the main house the next morning. Not a surprise there, as it is close to lunchtime by the time they both appear. The caterers have been and the kitchen has been restored to its usual casual chaos. The dismantled marquee is now in the process of being loaded onto a truck to the accompaniment of shouts and swearing. Ria and Shelley duck past the men and move inside where they find Aunt Kat in her office puzzling over the computer. With the ease of long practice Shelley moves to Aunt Kat's side and they immediately become engrossed in a discussion about the next function and the logistics involved. Ria seeing her presence is not required nor even noticed, quietly edges herself out of the room and heads back outside into the sunshine.

The rest of the day passes quickly for there are horses to be fed, brushed and played with. Starry the foal is a great time waster Ria decides. Not only is she happy to scratch and brush her, but there is also pleasure to be gained from just watching the foal interact with life around her – sniffing and exploring and scampering on still wobbly legs when startled.

It isn't until mid-afternoon that she returns to the main house where she finds her aunt and Shelley seated at the kitchen table eating biscuits and drinking tea, while consulting a cookbook and arguing over what to cook for dinner.

'No, Shelley. I insist it's my pleasure to cook dinner for you and the others,' her aunt says. 'You do enough here – more than you bargained for I expect. Let me look after you this once. You and Ria can wash up - how about that for an efficient distribution of labour? OK?'

'OK. Just this once,' Shelley murmurs.' But tomorrow it's my turn. Irish stew I think.'

'Oh no. Not again,' her aunt complains. 'Is that all you can cook?'

In the general laughter they do not hear the side door open. It is not until Aunt Kat's dog starts barking that they turn and notice the door slowly opening and a young woman entering the room. Aunt Kat abruptly stops laughing and with a hand clasped at her throat slowly rises from her chair. Ria and Shelley, remain silent, stay seated and watch the unfolding spectacle as if they were part of an audience watching a performance.

A young woman slowly enters the room and as she does, her head turns to and fro, gazing around as if looking for reassurance that she is in the right place. From her appearance, it is obvious she is Ben's sister, the mysterious Kitty. Strawberry blonde hair – a mass of wayward curls – a shorter slightly more tamed version of her brother's hairstyle. Fine features, eyes like the sea and an apprehensive expression. When she removes the stained baggy jacket, it becomes apparent that Kitty is bringing not just herself into the room, but that she is also the carrier of a young child – possibly seven months along in Ria's expert opinion.

Hesitantly the young woman approaches her mother, almost as if she is uncertain as to the reception she might receive. But she need not have worried. With a cry of delight Aunt Kat rushes forward, arms open wide and embraces her daughter.

'Kitty dear. Welcome back. It's been so long and I was so worried. How wonderful to have you back home. Here let me look at you.'

Stepping back, arms held out straight, but still gripping Kitty, Aunt Kat gazes at her daughter with affection, and then with puzzlement as she takes in the bulging tummy.

'My dear – you're pregnant?'

'Yes mum. It's a bit obvious isn't it,' said in a sarcastic tone and delivered in a world-weary manner. 'But I don't want to talk about it. I'm starving. Is there anything to eat?' All said as she disengages herself from her mother's clutches and heads to the table to sit next to Ria and Shelley. Clearly not expecting to see anyone else in the kitchen Kitty stares, flinty eyes appraising these other two young women.

'And who might you two be? I didn't know mum still had staff.'

'Kitty, that's enough,' warns Ben, having now entered the room behind his sister.

'Let me introduce you to Shelley, there on the end. Shelley helps mum with the functions and is visiting from Ireland. And this here is your cousin Ria who is visiting from Sydney.'

'Charmed I'm sure. Hope mum isn't working you too hard Shelley?' Turning to Ria Kitty continues, 'And a cousin? Ria you said? Well I never knew I had a cousin. Wow this is turning out to be a day full of surprises – dad dead and a new-found cousin. What else? How come I never knew of your existence Ria? We look like we might be contemporaries?'

Aunt Kat takes over the conversation. Speaking rapidly, almost as if she is feeling nervous she gives Kitty a quick summary of events to date – how she and Ria's mother had become estranged. In a few words she explains how Ria had made contact after her mother's death and had been welcomed into the family.

'How convenient,' Kitty drawls. 'Almost as if you had acquired a new daughter – and one that even looks like she belongs to this family. And how convenient for you Ria – I hope you are enjoying your new home. I'm sure it is a vast improvement on your old home – look around you. Not many places compete with this grand estate.'

Ria finds herself bristling. Did this bedraggled waif really mean to be so rude? Before she can get a word out Ben interrupts:

'You're clearly tired Kitty. I know it's been a long day, so I suppose that might be an excuse for your behaviour. Let's get you some dinner and then into bed.'

Before Kitty can protest, Shelley adds her bit.

'If you'll excuse us Kat, we'll go off to our cottage. I'm sure you have so much to talk about and you don't need us here to intrude. Come on Ria,' said while dragging Ria by the arm, so she has no choice but to stand upright and follow Shelley, who continues to hold her in a vicelike grip.

Once outside and out of earshot Ria hisses:

'What was that about? Why'd you do that?'

'Couldn't you see? It was obvious we were in the way. I think our life has just changed. Time for me to make plans to move on and I suspect your life is also going to become uncomfortable. Looks like Queen B doesn't like company.'

'What do you mean?'

'Don't you remember girls like her at school? She is clearly a bitch. An underfed and dirty bitch. Mark my words she is going to make our lives misery. I've seen people like her before. The only way you can save yourself is to run!'

'Surely not. She's my cousin.'

'Don't you know? Families are the worst!'

Chapter Thirteen

Next morning Ria wakes early, long before Shelley and makes her way apprehensively up to the big house. She finds her aunt sitting quietly at the kitchen table sipping a mug of tea. Gesturing at the teapot on the table it is clear she is inviting Ria to help herself. Once seated at the table by her aunt with a now steaming mug of tea in hand, Ria is uncertain as to how to start the conversation. She is dying to know what happened after she and Shelley left the previous night, but she doesn't know how to begin. Perhaps her uncertainty is clear in her expression as her aunt puts her out of her misery. Taking a further sip of her tea and then looking sadly at her niece Aunt Kat begins:

'I'm sorry about last night. No, there are no excuses,' she says in response to Ria's mumbled disclaimers.

'My daughter was just plain rude. Sure, she may have been tired and hungry, but really – how you saw her is just how she used to be. No change there – rude to anyone she thinks is a threat to her. She could be so horrible to Ben, you know, when she thought her father was favouring Ben over her. I had hoped she might have grown up and mellowed. That maybe life on the streets might have made her a bit more compassionate. But I doubt it. I'm sorry you had to see her this way. I'm hoping that this morning, once she has had a big rest and some decent food, things might be better. I'm really very sorry about last night. You and Shelley didn't deserve to be treated that way. I just hope you weren't too upset?'

Ria does her best to reassure her aunt and says how she has seen so much worse in her nursing career. But she is not sure that she has convinced her aunt.

'I suppose you're right. You must see all sorts in your line of work. I suppose it toughens you up – but still…'

Ben's arrival ends the now strained conversation. He bounces into the room, full of enthusiasm for the day and as he says: dying from hunger.

'Hey cuz fancy a ride this morning once I find some food? Any bacon and eggs ma? What with one thing and another I didn't get much dinner last night.'

Sometime later, now happily replete having consumed a full cooked breakfast they both wander over to the horse yards. Ben, aware he should also say something about the previous night, starts to apologise:

'Sorry about my sister last night. She can be a bit full on and I suppose a bit of a shock if you aren't used to her. I should've warned you, but I had kinda hoped she might have changed. You know, hoped maybe her recent experiences might have knocked the rough edges off her.'

'Your mum said something like that also. But it could be that is just the way your sister is. It's not that easy to change who we are. I hope that once we know each other better she might be more welcoming. It must have been a bit of a shock finding two strangers in the house.'

'You know what? You're too nice. Only child and all that. I suppose you've never had to deal with a sibling who always wanted to be number one. She'll see you as competition. Especially once she notices how fond my mother is of you. Don't worry though – I've got your back!'

'I'm a big girl. I can take care of myself. It's not your problem - really. I'm not worried at all!'

Well, actually I am. I don't want this so-called cousin Kitty to spoil the special bond that is developing with Ben, she thinks as she elbows her cousin, who immediately responds with a dig in her ribs and a ruffle of her hair. Arm in arm they wander into the yard and go to greet the now beloved Starry, who recognising them, watches their approach with curiosity.

Some time spent with foal and mother – Ria brushing and feeding Trixie, while Ben continues with Starry's education. The foal glossy with good health, nudges and rubs up against Ben as he tries to focus her attention.

'I think I will put the foal halter on her next time, not that I think she will have any issue with it. She is so used to being rubbed all over her face. But it's time she started to learn how to walk with a lead rope. She's a smart one just like her mother. I don't think there will be any issue about her learning. Come on,' he says to Ria, 'school's done for the day. Let's go for a ride. I have some water troughs to check.'

Another day, another wonderful ride on the oh so obedient Tonka. This time they ride out into the rough paddock where the cows are grazing. Ria cautiously skirts the cows, much to Ben's amusement. He assures her that the cattle, massive black animals with impressive horns, will pay her no mind, being totally at ease with horses. But Ria refuses to believe him. His teasing about pathetic city girls once again ensues. This time Ria agrees with him. There is no way she can be convinced that those black monsters don't mean her any harm.

Water troughs checked and found to be working with no leaks, their chores are done. Horses and riders amble back towards the stables, where they find a person waiting impatiently. It is Kitty, eyes flashing blue indignation.

'There you are at last and why is SHE on my horse?'

'Ah good morning Kitty,' Ben says amiably, as he brings Trixie to a halt and swings himself out of the saddle onto the ground.

'Well rested, are we?'

'Never mind that. You haven't answered my question. I don't let just anyone on Tonka. He has a very soft mouth you know, and I don't want him ruined. Here give him to me,' Kitty says dragging the reins from the hands off the now standing Ria who, having dismounted, was concentrating on running the stirrups up the leathers and preparing to undo Tonka's saddle. Ria hands the reins over without a comment, but with a puzzled look at Ben.

'Kitty. Enough. You haven't been here for years and life goes on without you, you know. Tonka needs riding and your cousin Ria is a very accomplished rider.' With a glance at Kitty's belly he continues, 'And in your current state, you've got buckleys of getting on this horse or even the smallest pony. Relax, he's in good hands. Just let Ria unsaddle Tonka and turn him out. Come with me and I'll show you our new foal. Starry we've called her. She's from one of dad's old brood mares and is a bit of a cutey.'

Just like a child, a bit of distraction works wonders with Kitty. Now focussed in seeing the foal, any contact with her old horse is no longer of any interest. Tonka's reins are thrust back into Ria's hands and with a muttered 'you take good care of him, you hear,' Kitty turns away and follows Ben to the far stable yard, where mare and foal await.

Ria busies herself with the unsaddling, washing and turning out of Tonka and then turns to do the same with Fidget who has been left tied up to a rail. All the while she can hear Ben's enthusiastic words in the distance. She just hopes his excitement will wash off on his sister. Ria is not sure how much more she can take of Kitty's bad attitude. Her tasks complete she wanders over to the yard towards Kitty and Ben. Somehow Ben has worked his magic – or it could be the foal who has changed things. For as she approaches, Ria can see an amazing change in her cousin – Kitty is a young woman transformed as she stands next to the foal and scratches Starry's neck under the spiky mane,. Laughing and relaxed, she radiates pleasure.

'She's gorgeous Ben. Can I have her when she is older. She'd be perfect for my baby. Please…' large eyes look beseechingly at Ben.

He laughs.

'There's no rush. Your sprog will only need a pony for years to come, not one like this miss, who will mature to a fair size. But don't panic. We're keeping her. Who knows, she might be a good riding horse for you?'

As they wander back to the house Ria finds it hard to relate to this changed Kitty. Brightly smiling and chattering away about nothing, she includes both Ben and Ria in the conversation. At first, feeling rather wary of her cousin Ria restricts her responses, but soon she finds herself being cross examined about her past and resigns herself to divulging more than she would prefer to.

'Yes. I grew up in Sydney. In Glebe. My mum lived with her godmother, Penny. Your mum knows Penny I think. No. I didn't know you or your mum or Ben existed until after mum died. When did she die? Recently. And I then thought I should come and meet this mysterious family. When am I going home? I don't know – probably soon.

By this time, it is clear to Ben that Ria is not appreciating the grilling she is receiving from Kitty and as earlier, he successfully employs the distraction technique.

'Come on sis. Let's give our cousin a break. You go back to the house Ria and I'll show my curious sister my latest sculpture. Come on this way little, or not so little sister,' he says, casting a cautious eye over Kitty's burgeoning stomach. Linking his arm through Kitty's he leads her away over to his workshop. With a sigh of relief Ria continues towards the house.

I'm not sure I can cope with this, she thinks.

Chapter Fourteen

Over the following few days life continues to be unsettled. Ria, despite doing her best to remain calm and gracious, constantly feels on edge. She notices her aunt also seems to be suffering. It appears they are all held hostage to Kitty's moods. One moment all will be fine. Kitty will be exuberantly interested in whatever is happening and offering to lend a hand in the latest activity. Then the next moment without any apparent change in circumstances or events, her voice would be raised and, with door slamming, Kitty would bolt from the room in a temper, but not before some vindictive words would have been said, mostly directed at Ria. For some reason, Ria was often the focus of any spiteful diatribe. Shelley was largely ignored. Ben made himself absent, pleading an urgent need to help Geordie over on his farm. So, it was left to Aunt Kat to try and make the peace – with limited success.

'I'm not sure what's got into her. She always was a handful, but never this cranky. Maybe it's the pregnancy, but when I ask her anything about it she just snaps my head off,' says an increasingly worried Kat.

'Aunt, it's early days. Who knows what impact her time away has had on her. It must take a while for her to settle back into home after all that Kitty must have been through. And then on top of that, to hear the news about her father. That must have been a shock for her. You said they were close?'

'Yes. They were. Ben told her the news on the drive back home, but when I tried to talk to Kitty about it the next morning, she just brushed me aside. Said she didn't want to talk about it. Said he was gone, that he was a bastard and that was that. Just so hard to understand. Surely, she would grieve? I certainly am.'

Both aunt and niece are silent as each contemplates the misery that is death by suicide. Aunt Kat's expression is closed and grim, not inviting any confidences. Yet Ria, aware she may not get another opportunity to find out what had happened to Uncle Mick loses no time and dives right in. This might be the only moment to get her aunt to talk about what happened.

'Aunt,' says Ria taking her aunt's calloused workworn hand in hers. 'I'm so sorry I never got the chance to meet my uncle. If it isn't too painful would you mind telling me about him and your life together? You must have been very young when you met? I mean Ben is only a little bit older than me, so you must have been a young bride and then a young mum.'

No need for any further encouragement. Like a dam bursting, the words tumble out. There is no stopping Aunt Kat in her eagerness to share the memories with anyone who might listen. Her eyes soften and glow as she remembers happier times. A vibrancy comes into her voice and her manner as she relives that time, not so long ago.

'Yes, I was young. Mind you I had always known Mick. He grew up here on the farm and I was in the village, but we went to different schools. He went to the posh grammar school in town and I was at the public high school. However, our parents were friends, so there were many social opportunities for us to meet and mingle. When I was little, we used to play in the garden while our parents played tennis and then, as we got older, we were the ones playing tennis, while the oldies sat on the lawn and gossiped. I had always hero worshipped him, but it wasn't until I was about 17 that I think he even noticed me in that way, and not as an annoying little brat that would follow him around like a shadow. Then one thing led to another and – well - our families were delighted when we got married. Ben came soon after and then Kitty quite a few years later. They were busy times and like all marriages we had our good times and our bad. But overall we were happy – or so I thought.'

'You thought?'

'He was a bit like Kitty you see. A bit moody. When he was happy he could charm the birds out of the trees – he was so .... what's the word?'

'Magnetic?'

'Yes, that's it. But when Mick was in a bad mood he was best to be avoided. He was a hard man in many ways. It was his way or no way, and he could be very forceful. I tried to keep out of his way when he was like that and the kids did too – even Kitty. Of course, like the rest of us Mick was devastated when Kitty ran away, but I thought he was coping – getting on with life like we all had to. By then his moods were pretty bad, but I didn't have any concerns he might behave as he did. I just managed as usual – kept out of his way and hoped it would blow over. Maybe I should've tried to talk to him. Yet at that time I was barely managing myself, so I'm not sure I would have been much use. And then one day he went out to the back paddock with the shot gun and – well you can guess the rest.' Kat looked down at her hands as she fought against the threatening tears. Then, taking a deep breath she continued:

'I suppose the hardest thing was not knowing why he did it. He left no note you see. People kept asking if there were financial issues. Sure, things were tight, but then farming always is a challenge – but we were managing. I still don't get it. Nevertheless, I have had to learn to accept that there is so much I will never know about my husband or what he was thinking. Since then I have tried to make a life for Ben and for myself – I owe Ben that. But still there are days when I feel the grief pulling me under. I suppose when he killed himself Mick had no thought for how it would affect the rest of us – or didn't care.'

'I'm really sorry Aunt,' Ria said, while cuddling the now weeping Aunt Kat. 'I wish mum and I had been here and had been able to help you. You've had to deal with so much on your own. I'm so sorry we weren't here for you.'

'Well you are here now and Ria dear. I do appreciate it.' Aunt Kat draws a crumpled handkerchief from out of her pocket, wipes her eyes and then with a forceful honk blows her nose. 'Meeting you has been an absolute delight. Almost like having your mother back here with me – although you are so much calmer than she ever was. I'm just sorry my girl isn't more welcoming, and I do hope that will change someday soon, for I would hate to lose you again.'

Giving her aunt another quick hug Ria does her best to reassure her, telling her she has dealt with all sorts during her nursing career and a bit of a challenge never hurt anyone.

Yet later that evening after experiencing another bout of temperament from her cousin, Ria is not so sure. As soon as they can, she and Shelley take the opportunity to make their excuses and head back to the cottage for an early night.

'I'm not sure I will be staying for much longer,' confides Shelley. 'Things here are becoming a bit too uncomfortable and I think it is time I headed north for a wee break before I look for further work. What about you?'

'I know what you mean. I had planned to stay for a while longer and probably should stay to help Aunt Kat, especially if you are leaving. I don't know for sure. I still have some leave left before I need to return to work, but now I don't know. Things have changed here, and not for the better.'

Ria's daily attempts to be friendly with her newfound cousin are a challenge. On a good day, when Kitty is bubbly and excited with the joy of living and the imminent arrival of her baby, she draws Ria in and includes her into conversation as she shares with Ria her plans for the future. Kitty talks of a life on the farm bringing up her child surrounded by animals and in bucolic contentment. Kitty takes it for granted that her vision of the future includes Ria in a role of pseudo-sister and joint participant in all her anticipated adventures. On a bad day Ria's very existence attracts ire and muttered comments about certain visitors overstaying their welcome. If Aunt Kat or Ben take Kitty to task about her rudeness, all that results is a muttered *whatever* and a retreat by Kitty to her bedroom.

It was inevitable that the situation would come to a head and so it does one weekend. Ria and Shelley had been busy setting up the rooms for the birthday function to be held there the next day. As it was to be an afternoon tea, various small tables to seat four or six had been set up in the old ball room. Now covered in fine linen table clothes that had been embroidered by some distant relative years ago they made the room resemble an English tearoom in some quaint tourist town. That afternoon Ria was busy setting out the fine china – cups, saucers and plates, while Shelley was focussing on distributing cake forks and locating teaspoons. Each cup and saucer, being of a different pattern attracted Ria's admiring attention, which she then shared with Shelley. They were not making much progress with their tasks, as there was always a new pattern or hand painted technique to be admired on the various cups and saucers. With laughter and chatter they failed to notice the noise of approaching footsteps, until two burly men stomp into the room.

'Hey you two. What's up? We could hear you from outside. Giving the chooks a bit of competition with your cackling!' laughs Ben, as he nudges Geordie in the ribs.

'And welcome to you too! Such a pleasure to see such charming people. If only we had made some tea you could sample some of these beautiful tea cups.'

'Well, it's wasted on us. We've come to drag you off to the pub. Come on. I've spoken to mum. You can leave this for tomorrow morning. Let's get going before she changes her mind.'

Fun though setting up the fine china and cutlery was, it was certainly no competition against the chance of an outing. Ria could see that Shelley was desperate to go out for a bit of fun and for that matter, Ria was eager to see Ben who had been mysteriously absent the last few days. The added attraction of Geordie was an even better reason to go. Not stopping to change they are off and in the car before Ria becomes aware of Kitty's absence.

'What about Kitty? Is she going to join us?'

'I doubt it,' says Ben while glancing across at Geordie, who is seated in the front passenger seat. 'She was resting and I didn't like to disturb her. Anyway, I suspect associating with all the local plebs down at the pub is not her idea of fun.'

Just like the last time they visited, the pub is a mass of people, laughing and gossiping and of course – drinking. Like last time they stand out the front on the footpath and are soon joined by others. Local news is shared, triumphs exclaimed over and failures mourned. The same as any other night really, until Ria hears Ben muttering under his breath:

'Oh, oh. Here's trouble.'

Ria looks in the direction of Ben's glance and sees her cousin Kitty approaching. Or maybe it should be more accurately described as sashaying, like a model down the catwalk. Dressed in an indigo flowing shirt over black leggings, her pregnancy is not so obvious. The blue of the shirt brings out the colour in her eyes and provides a strong counterpoint to her coppery red gold hair. A glowingly clean Kitty, who is almost unrecognisable from the girl who arrived such a short time ago. As Kitty slowly approaches, the heads turn to observe this stunning woman, that has seemingly just appeared from out of nowhere. Their eyes widen in speculation, muttered whispers are shared, as those in the know, identify this stranger and share their knowledge with the others. If Kitty is aware of the attention she is attracting she gives no indication but just continues with her approach. Drawing near she greets Ben and Ria with a hello and a request – no a command – to be introduced.

Ben does the honours and introduces Kitty to all those standing around one by one, until he comes to Geordie.

'And of course, you remember Geordie?'

'Yes, yes I do. Hi Geordie. I thought you might have already come to see me as I'm sure Ben would have told you I'd returned.' Turning to Ria, who is doing her best to look politely interested, she adds while smiling archly: 'Geordie and I go a long way back. Almost since we were little we were an item. Remember Geordie how you promised to marry me when you were older? I think I was 8 at the time, but already you had decided I was the one. So sweet it was. So sorry I had to run off like I did – but maybe we can pick up where we left off? I seem to recall you were very keen at that time?'

'Kitty,' hisses Ben, 'this is not the time for your games. Can't you see no-one is interested?' he says pointing at the crowd, who sensing discord, are slipping away towards other groupings. 'Give it a break.'

Kitty glancing at Geordie who, by now, is looking rather anguished and then, as she glances at Ria, she continues:

'Fickle Geordie. I can see you haven't been pining for me at all. And I'd had such high hopes. You're clearly after new flesh. Well, at least you're keeping it in the family, although I don't think much of your taste – unless you fancy wimpy girls!'

Ben, now grabbing Kitty by the arm, drags her away.

'Come on you. I'm taking you home before you do any more damage. What's with you? Can't you say anything nice?'

With a muttered aside to Geordie to bring Ria and Shelley home at some stage, Ben leaves, dragging a still protesting Kitty away. She can still be heard as they head up the footpath.

'What did I do? I was just trying to make conversation. You can't deny Geordie and I were once an item and I thought he still cared for me. After all the promises he made, you would've thought he could remain faithful …' Her voice fades away, but not before the damage is done.

Geordie stands quietly beside Ria looking like someone who has been stunned into silence. Then, with a shake of his head and an anxious look at Ria, he starts to speak and try to explain.

'I'm sorry you had to hear that. I don't know what has got into her. Ben said things had been difficult, but I hadn't realised how bad things have been. I'm really sorry, but it seems like you and I are both unpopular.'

'Well, I'm certainly often in the firing line. I think my mere presence on the farm is what annoys her. But you? What happened? It's like she considers you two to still be a couple…'

'We were never a couple!' Geordie interjects. 'Sure, I might have said something foolish to her when we were kids, but that cannot count for anything other than childhood affection. You know we almost grew up as brother and sister and I was very fond of her then. And maybe we did have a couple of dates in that year just before she ran away, but there was never anything in it – or at least there never was for me. Even then she was too demanding and even a bit scary.'

He reaches out a hand and with an almost pleading look in his eyes continues: 'Please don't get the idea we were a couple. We never were. Kitty's just making mischief as she can see I like you. She never wants to see anyone happy.'

Ria shakes her head and puzzles over what she has just heard. So, her cousin causes trouble and is most likely jealous of her – well, that comes as no surprise. But then the other part of what Geordie said registers in her thinking. *He likes me? Really?* Now that is something of a surprise, but not an unwelcome one. Her hand now snakes out to reach his. Hands clasp; they gaze at each other. One gazing anxiously, as if his soul has been laid bare and could be open to injury. The other gazing in wonder, as if she has just discovered some unhoped-for wish is about to come true.

'You mean it? Really? You like ME?'

'Of course I do. Who wouldn't. I bet half the people at the pub tonight fancy you. Possibly even your cousin come to that, but just focus on me and forget all the others. Let's get out of here. No, we can't. I've forgotten Shelley. Where is she?'

Shelley, it appears has no intention of leaving. Finally tracked down to a discreet corner near the bar, she's busy forming an attachment with another young farmer.

With a waved dismissal her intentions are evident.

'No, it's grand here. Don't worry about me. I'll get myself home, by and by. Off with you now.'

She waves them goodbye and then turns back to the young man, intent on resuming their intimate conversation.

Slowly and side by side Ria and Geordie walk away from the noisy pub up the wide street towards Geordie's car. Now silent and uncertain as to what to say after Geordie's true confession, they both appear to be struggling with how to find words to continue the conversation. The uncomfortable moment extends. Two sets of eyes look forward, two bodies walking in step, yet apart. Until, as if driven by the same unspoken command and at the same moment, together they turn and face each other. Hands reach out and clasp. Bodies lean in. Ria's head tilts forward, to rest on his chest: she is so much shorter than he is after all. For a moment she stands still, just like that, leaning in and resting, seeking and receiving comfort from the physical strength of this man. Then reaching up, stretching onto her tiptoes she lifts her face up to his. They kiss – butterfly kisses at first, and then, with increasing intensity, the kisses deepen as bodies and emotions are explored. At last, breathless with relief and laughter, they break free and gaze at each other with wonder.

'Enough – well enough for now. Let's get out of here before we attract the local police constable's attention,' says Geordie, pushing Ria towards his car.

Once seated in the car there's no rush to start the engine. Focus instead is on each other as they resume the kissing, the cuddling and the fondling of each other.

Ria, lost in the sensations thinks of nothing else, but the pleasure she is giving and receiving. All thoughts of recent conflict fall away as she focuses on all her senses. *So long*, she thinks. *It feels like forever since I have felt like this. Why did I leave it so long?*

Somehow, they have sufficient focus to start the car and head back out of the village. At Ria's suggestion, they drive back to *Kings View*, for as she explains Shelley will be out until much later and they will have the cottage to themselves. Geordie drives slowly, talking to Ria about this and that. Ria adds her bit, all the while her hand resting protectively on his muscled thigh. This sudden rush into intimacy at once so disconcerting yet also feeling so right, as if she has known Geordie for ever and not just for a few weeks.

Back at the cottage, the fire lit and a simple supper of scrambled eggs prepared, they sit on cushions before the now roaring open fire and try to fill in the gaps in their knowledge of each other. From such different backgrounds and yet, somehow, they connect. Geordie from a farming family who have been settled in the same location for generations. Farming he tells her, is in his blood and even if he could, he has never wanted to move away from this life. Never any wish to go to university or to try any other career, he tells her he is happiest when he is outside on his beloved farm and with his animals. Although, he tells her, his broad smile also reflected in his eyes, this could now be subject to change, given his new interest in a certain young city girl. Ria agrees that she, as a city girl would never have anticipated being involved with a farmer. In fact, she concedes, because of her nursing career, she always thought she would end up with a doctor or another nurse – they being the only people she ever mixed with. Patients were in and out in no time, so it wasn't possible to form any strong connection with them and the guests in her mother's BnB were nearly always couples. Unless she fancied a threesome, and she confesses sometimes that was on offer, there was never any hope for a proper romance. But now, she laughs at him, she has discovered another life and a whole world of new interests. All thanks to her mother, who finally revealed the truth about her family and whose revelations brought her here.

Much later, lying in bed, safely in the security of Geordie's arms, Ria contemplates what she has just shared with this amazing man lying by her side.

'Did I just imagine it? Are you really here – in my bed?'

'Well it depends on your imagination I suppose,' says Geordie reaching across and pulling Ria close. She settles into his body and hooks her leg over his. One hand casually strokes his chest and then trails down the fine line of hair that leads below.

'Careful! You might just be starting something there that you might regret!'

'Might I? Sounds like a dare to me. So, if I just keep on going what will happen?'

'Your dreams will come true!'

'Modest, aren't you? Go on then. Show me!'

And he does.

Much, much later just before she drifts off into blissful unconsciousness, Ria counts her blessings and sends a message of gratitude to her mother, wherever she may be.

Chapter Fifteen

A splashing noise, a sensation of damp and cold and Ria is jolted awake. It is daylight and she is dripping wet.

The man who had been lying next to her in the bed, squirms and abruptly sits upright. Similarly wet, he is busy shaking soaked hair out of his eyes.

A screaming, like that of so many furious seagulls engulfs them. The words, initially a blur of sound now can be clearly understood.

'You bitch. He's mine. I told you that last night, but did you pay any attention? No! You had to go after him like some alley cat in heat. Well, I've taken care of you just like a feral cat you are. You've had your soaking – so scram. Get outa here. Go back to the Sydney slums where you belong! Here's a bit more to focus your thinking.'

And with that further water is hurled in Ria's direction, soaking both her and Geordie and the bed. Now awake they both stare at the outraged vision before them, Ria clutching a sopping sheet to her chest. Even in such dire circumstances modesty must be preserved. She watches this screaming banshee at the foot of the bed, wondering how Kitty even knew Geordie was here. At the same time, her professional training is telling her that this is a seriously disturbed person, who must be somehow calmed before she does harm to herself, to her baby or to them.

Brain slipping into gear she finds herself agreeing with Kitty. 'Kitty. Of course. But give me time to get changed, and then we'll sort things out. I'm a bit wet you see, and I need to get these sheets in the washing machine. You could help me, you know?'

The glazed look of fury fades and, as Ria hoped, Kitty is distracted. Like a child she now focuses on the next issue and seemingly forgets the trauma provoked by the sight of Ria and Geordie in bed together.

'Help? How?' The eyes brighten with the thought of a new challenge.

'Well you see Geordie hasn't had breakfast. Do you think you could go see if you and Aunt Kat can make him something? He's starving. He'll be up in a minute.'

Ria refrains from mentioning Geordie's state of undress, as she fears it might further inflame Kitty. But her distraction ploy has worked. A new Kitty, a happily engaged Kitty, agrees to help prepare breakfast and bustles away, the front door slamming behind her.

'You did well there, Ria. For just a moment I thought we were at risk of injury,' says Geordie, the relief apparent in his expression.

'Well, actually that wasn't the way I'd hoped to wake up this morning! But seriously. I'm worried that this is more than just bad behaviour or jealousy, and that Kitty is seriously disturbed. I need to get up to the house and talk to my aunt. Are you OK to go along with the performance and enjoy your breakfast?'

Bed stripped, wet sheets in washing machine and doona hung over the fence to dry, the still jittery couple head cautiously up the path to the house.

'I'm worried about this Ria. I'm not sure you're safe here. Who knows what will happen next time. Life here just seems to be ramping up.'

'Yeah it is. I mean it has been verbal abuse up to now, but this morning is the first time there's been any form of assault. All this distress can't be good for any of us – especially for Kitty. And it can't be good for the baby.'

Up at the house it is as if nothing has occurred. Aunt Kat, unaware of the drama, greets Ria and Geordie with smiling good humour.

'Good morning you two. Kitty tells me you're after breakfast. Let me get something cooking – will bacon and eggs do?'

'Please Mrs Kingsley. That would be delicious.'

'How many times do I have to tell you Geordie. It's Kat.'

'Sorry. It's a habit. All those years of calling you Mrs K when I was a child. Old habits die hard. But OK. Kat, it is. And bacon and eggs would be a treat. Let me help you.'

For some reason after the events of that morning and with her stomach now in full churn, the last thing Ria can contemplate is a hearty breakfast. Once Geordie is busy tucking into a full plate of food under the intense supervision of Kitty, Ria seizes the opportunity to speak to her aunt alone. Using the excuse of checking the set up in the ballroom as a diversion, she escorts her rather puzzled aunt away.

As soon as they are out of earshot Ria explains what has happened that morning and shares with her aunt her concerns about the emotional wellbeing of Kitty.

'Surely not,' expostulates her aunt. 'She's just a bit excitable that's all.'

'No aunt. It's more than that. Kitty was so hysterical at the pub last night that Ben had to bring her home. And then this morning when she threw water over Geordie and me she was still beside herself.'

'Maybe it was her idea of a joke. Look at her now. Happy and calm. I find it hard to believe anything like that happened. Are you sure you're not exaggerating a bit? And anyway, why is Geordie here? I thought he was sweet on Kitty. If you've gone and stolen him off my girl, no wonder things have got tense.'

With a sense of foreboding Ria realises her aunt, for whatever reason, is refusing to believe anything she has just told her. Or even to listen to what she is trying to say. Her aunt turns towards the tables now neatly set in preparation for the upcoming afternoon tea. Moving swiftly, she fusses over the settings – moving first one cup and saucer and now another, repositioning spoons and cake forks until, with a nod of her head, she is now satisfied with the infinitesimal changes she has wrought.

'Now, that's better. A few flowers on the side tables and we will be ready for this afternoon.'

For a moment, all is as it has been in recent weeks. The quietly efficient Aunt Kat focussed on the task at hand in her usual calm no-nonsense manner. But then a change as she turns towards Ria. Her expression has changed – determined and stern, the blue eyes flinty. It is clear Aunt Kat is in command.

'Don't get me wrong Ria. It's been a pleasure having you stay, but I think it is time you left. I don't know what's going on, but I can tell your being here is not good for my Kitty – especially if you have stolen her man. After all she is my daughter and is my responsibility. Don't forget your being here was meant to be just a visit. It's not your home and you really have no reason to stay. You've met us and you now know we exist, but your life is elsewhere. It might be best for all concerned if you go and pack your stuff. There's a train back to Sydney at lunchtime. I'll take you to the station. That way you won't need to bother anyone or upset Kitty any further.'

Just like a bag of rubbish, she was being packed up and moved out of sight before anyone became aware of how much she was on the nose. For all her aunt's earlier loving words, Ria was beginning to understand that she would always be considered an outsider and never part of the family. The camaraderie of recent weeks, the bonding over hard work and disasters which she thought had reflected genuine affection, had just been a façade. Ria stares blankly at her aunt who returns the stare with grim purpose.

'Like I said. Go and pack and I'll give your excuses to Geordie.'

'Aunt, please don't do this. I can help. You need my help. Believe me. Kitty needs to see a doctor. I'm seriously worried about her and she needs medical treatment before she puts the baby at risk.'

It's all Ria can do to get these words out as her tears threaten to overwhelm her. But to no avail. Her aunt is adamant.

'Well, I'm her mother and I'm not worried. Of course, Kitty is a bit over excitable, but that is all. She's always been that way inclined. You nurses are all the same. You always exaggerate – trying to make work for yourself. Well, you won't succeed this time young lady. I've got your measure. Off you go,' and with a shove, Ria is pushed out the door onto the veranda. 'I'll come and find you shortly, so don't think you can avoid me.'

A short while later Ria is seated on her bed, open suitcase beside her. Her head in a whirl, she has made no attempt to start packing. Her aunt's words play over and over in her head, to her increasing distress. When she hears the front screen door slam, her heart lifts as she thinks it might be Geordie come to sort things out. But as the familiar smiling face of Shelley peeps around the door she realises it is not to be. Shelley, her entire being aglow and replete with the contentment that only a romantic encounter can bring, wafts into the room high on the cloud of her own happiness. So happy is she, that for a moment Shelley fails to take in the slumped figure on the bed before her and the empty suitcase beside Ria. Then the reality hits.

'Hey Ria, what's happening? Has something happened at home? You look terrible. It's not your Penny, is it?'

'No,' Ria sighs. 'It's a long story and I still can't work out what happened. I feel like I'm trapped in a horrible nightmare. I keep waiting for someone to wake me up, but it's not happening. And I had such hopes for today ….' Her voice trails off as she contemplates the misery that is her existence.

At Shelley's prompting Ria relates the events of that morning. Shelley's horrified reaction is confirmation that the behaviour of Aunt Kat is bizarre. They both agree that Kitty's conduct is clearly unhinged – but Aunt Kat?

'She can't do that, can she? Just kick you out?'

'Yes, of course she can. It's her home after all. It's just – well it doesn't make sense. I thought I was welcome. And I haven't even had a chance to speak to Geordie or to Ben,' Ria's voice increases in volume and ends in a sob.

Shelley is now on the warpath, her Irish temper coming to the fore.

'Never you mind about that. You stay right here and I'll go and see if I can find them. I bet they're both up at the stables – I suspect they'll be giving Kitty a wide berth. Leave it to me,' the last words said over her shoulder, as Shelley bustles out the door and then outside.

Ria has never seen Shelley so energised – like a pocket dynamo. Maybe she should have gone into battle with Aunt Kat on her behalf? If she had would the outcome be any different? But then with a sigh, Ria lies back on the still damp mattress and ponders her fate. The harsh reality was that for the last few weeks she had been living in a world that was not meant to be. This had never been her home and never would be. Despite her growing love for the farm, its animals and the joys of rural living, she had no claim to this part of the world, other than a hope that occasionally she could, as a relative, be invited to visit. And even then, she had no control over when or how long she could stay. She would always be the guest, only involved in farm life when the owners consented and only allowed to stay for as long as she was permitted.

Now her time was up. Unless circumstances changed it was unlikely she would ever be invited to return. That this could be her one and only visit to *Kings View* felt devastating, like a future vision of a contented life, which had been once so temptingly laid out before her and was now being snatched away. No more early morning rides on Tonka, no more cosy times spent with Ben, teasing and laughing over some cousinly rivalry and no more times spent peacefully in the company of her aunt out in the garden. No point in even thinking about the romance that had started so promisingly the night before. A long-distance love affair was doomed to fail.

It was time to behave like an adult and return to her reality, which once, before she came to *Kings View*, had seemed so fulfilling and had been all she had ever wanted. Now that an alternative way of living had presented itself to her, Ria realised that city living was no longer for her. Yet, she had no choice but to return – to Glebe and to Penny - to her old ways and to her old job. She could only hope that once back at her home it might be possible to put all the dreams of this amazing life behind her. If only it didn't feel so hard – like forcing herself into clothing that no longer fitted. It was fine once, but it no longer did it for her.

She hears voices and footsteps approaching down the path. The door slams, then three people surge into her soon to be vacated bedroom. Ben and Geordie squeeze next to her on the bed, their faces etched with concern. Shelley stands by the doorway. The small room now feels overcrowded and pulsing with emotion.

'Ria, Shelley just told me what happened. Are you alright?' asks Geordie, taking her hand in his.

Ria just nods and sniffs.

'I don't understand it,' exclaims Ben, running his hands through his already bedraggled hair. 'I tried to talk to mum, but she told me her mind was made up and that this was for the best. As if! She then told me to go away,' the last sentence said in a tone of disbelief. 'She's never said that to me before! I just don't get it.' His voice stumbles to a halt, as he contemplates Ria with a look full of as much misery as she also feels.

Ever the carer Ria feels the need to help both her cousin, and Geordie, who still holding her hand just watches her silently, waves of concern emanating from him.

'It's OK. Well no. It's not OK, but maybe Aunt Kat is right – maybe it's for the best if I go back home for a little while and give everyone a bit of space. That way Kitty might settle. For some reason, my being here seems to set her off. Like I'm a threat or something. Maybe with time she might come to see me differently.'

'Or maybe not,' mutters Ben. 'It could be she resents how you've become part of the family. I sometimes think you seem more like a sister to me and more like a daughter to mum than Kitty. You settled in here straightaway, like you were born to it. Unlike Kitty, who hates the place. It's almost as if you were meant to live here.' Shaking his head, hair in disarray like a wild shaking mop, he continues, 'I won't give up. You belong here. So, I'll put you on the train today but don't get too settled in the big smoke. Geordie and I will come and drag you back – that's both a promise and a threat!'

With the help of her friends Ria's possessions are soon in the two suitcases that not so long ago she had brought with her from Sydney. Like the unwanted visitor she now is, the boys escort her up to the car which they have parked near the cottage and away from the house. They assure her there is no need to say goodbye to her aunt or to Kitty – telling her it is best if she slips away unnoticed. Ria is inclined to disagree, but to do so would take more energy than she can currently muster. It is taking all her reserves to disengage herself from a now weeping Shelley.

'I'm sorry, but I can't stop crying. I can't believe this is happening. We were having such fun sharing the cottage – not quite sisters, but just about. I'm going to miss you so. The joy's gone out of it - somehow. You know, I rather think you might see me in Sydney very soon.'

Ria has never been one for farewells and the fraught emotions she has just experienced with Shelley do not set her up well for further leave-takings at the railway station. Perhaps the boys also feel this way or perhaps they are just displaying that male characteristic of avoiding emotional scenes. But whatever the reason, the boys are now strangely silent. Ria and suitcases deposited on the railway platform, Ben removes himself with a muttered excuse about buying a ticket for Ria, leaving Geordie standing side by side with Ria. The train is due very soon, so there is little time for chat. Yet Ria doesn't know what to say. Last night had been everything she had hoped it would be. Geordie, caring, passionate and funny had made the night memorable and she had hoped there would be other occasions. Now she is not so sure. Maybe it was just a one off – a one-night stand? Geordie's voice intrudes into her thoughts.

'You know. I've been thinking as we drove here that it might be for the best if we just chilled for a bit?'

'What do you mean – chilled?' asks Ria, a feeling of dread engulfing her. Was the joy she experienced last night a one-sided experience. Surely, he had felt it too?

Taking her hands in his massive paws Geordie speaks slowly as if he is talking to someone who is a bit slow on the uptake, and perhaps in her current state of shock, that is what Ria has become.

'You don't need the pressure of trying to manage a relationship with someone so far away. Maybe if you had stayed here a while longer we would have had time to get to know each other better. Then we might have had a chance. Admit it. It's not going to work Ria – whatever we have – had – never had a chance to get off the ground and now it's too late. I am stuck here. I can't just leave the farm every weekend to see you. Life doesn't work that way. Who knows - one day when things calm down and you can return? Then maybe?'

With an increasing sense of unreality Ria shakes her head as if trying to clear her thoughts. She cannot believe what she has just heard. Then anger surges through her veins. How dare he!

'No – don't waste your time. No maybes. If you can't be bothered even trying to maintain some contact, then you aren't the person I thought you were. Was I too *easy* for you? No point in trying to build a relationship. I see it now – you just wanted a one night stand. Well, you got that so – so you can now go. NOW!' Ria's voice chokes with emotion – rage battling with grief welling up from her very being. How had this gone so wrong?

Geordie, shoulders slumped turns and walks away, passing the now returning Ben.

'What's happening? Why's Geordie going and why does he look so miserable? Have you dumped him? I thought you liked him?'

'Ben. He dumped me!' sobs now making Ria's voice unintelligible, but somehow Ben discerns her meaning. He reaches for her and pulls Ria in close to his chest, where tears and snot leave their mark.

'Hey steady on. This is a clean shirt you know. And I don't have many of those.'

'Sorry,' a tear-stained face is raised to his.

'Look I have an idea. No, no need to look hopeful just yet. This day has been a complete disaster. Let's just put it behind us, get you on this train and get you home to Sydney. Your cousin Ben, the clairvoyant of the family, predicts things will improve once people calm down. Hey, it can't get much worse, can it?'

A watery chuckle greets this attempt at humour but is quickly subsumed by more wracking sobs.

'Oh, Ben what will I do?'

'You'll carry on, just, like the rest of us and trust that things will improve. Don't say I didn't tell you this family was trouble! You were warned. Look here's the train now. Get on and I'll talk to you soon. Hold onto that thought. This could be just another of those road bumps in life. Well, more than one road bump, but you can take it. Look what you've dealt with so far. I have faith in my new best friend. Come on now – wipe your eyes and get going.'

Best friend? He said best friend? I'm his best friend? His words repeat over and over in Ria's mind. Who would have thought this gorgeous, yet scruffy cousin would now consider her as his best friend? Maybe something good has come out of this visit after all – and that in time she might be able to redeem herself with Aunt Kat and Kitty and somehow resurrect the romance that had started so promisingly the night before?

Over the following hours, as the train traverses the countryside, the vague optimism that Ria so briefly felt when she farewelled Ben, slowly dissipates. By the time the train starts to slow with the approach of the outer suburbs of Sydney, she feels just plain miserable. As if in harmony with her mood, the weather outside darkens and rain begins to fall. Not a misty, romantically comforting rain, but a torrential take no prisoners tropical downpour.

There had been no time to alert Penny to her unexpected return. A very surprised Penny only became aware that her beloved girl had returned, when she opened the door to a half-drowned waif: the water dripping from Ria's head combining with the tears that now flow down her drenched face.

Penny opens her arms, just like she did all those years ago when she opened the door to Ria's mother Bianca.

'Oh, you poor dear. What happened to you? Come in. Let me get you dry. Look at you. You're soaked, like a half-drowned rat.'

Just like before, the young woman at the door hurls herself into Penny's arms, choking and shuddering with sobs. As before, all Penny could do was hold this quivering body and murmur words of comfort. For now, that would have to do.

Chapter Sixteen

1975 – Penny and Bianca

Many years later, in one of her rare contemplative moments Penny would marvel at how, in a split second, her life had completely changed, just by the act of opening her front door in response to a hesitant knock.

Before she opened that door, her life had been predictably staid. A lecturer, whose vocation was her passionate devotion to the study of history. No time for a partner and no need to be lonely with the regular churn in her life brought about by a series of energetic student boarders. Her life was full, her brain completely occupied, and she had no wish for anything other than what she already had.

Then she opened the front door and all was transformed. As she stood in the doorway gazing at the sodden child before her, Penny briefly wondered if the child was another student wanting accommodation. But when the child looked her full in the face, she immediately knew who it was.

Bianca, her goddaughter stood before her. Clearly distressed and certainly in need of drying and possibly comforting.

'My dear child. You're soaking. Come in. Let's get you changed and in front of the heater. Or maybe you need a hot shower to warm you up? Yes, that might be better. While you do that I'll find you some dry clothes, but be warned they'll probably swim on you. However, they'll have to do for now until I can get your stuff dry. Come on, this way.'

As Penny led her through the doorway and down the wide corridor, Bianca glanced around. The house built in the mid-19th century for some aspiring merchant, still resonated with pretensions of grandeur. The wide corridor leading past an impressive cedar staircase provided an imposing opening statement. Glimpses to right and left revealed two ornate rooms just inside the front door, now furnished rather casually: one as a sitting room and the other as a dining room. Past the stairs they followed the corridor out to the back of the house to where a combined kitchen/sitting room were located in an enormous glassed-in veranda. So obviously the heart of the house where much of the living took place, as evidenced by the array of magazines and books scattered on kitchen counters and in piles beside shabby lounge chairs. Through the windows she could see a small, paved garden sheltered by a massive lacy-leaved tree. She would later learn this tree was a jacaranda, the subject of many curses as she constantly swept up the discarded purple blossoms that rained onto the ground every summer. Across that paved yard another building, the restored coach house, which she soon discovered provided sleeping space and refuge for her and Penny, away from the cacophony of the student boarders.

Penny bustled into an adjoining room, which must be a bathroom, as she returned with an enormous striped towel.

'Here wrap this around you and go in there,' she said, pointing to the room from which she had just exited. 'Hop into the shower and warm up, while I go find some clothes for you and some slippers too, I suppose. I'll leave the clothes outside the door for when you are ready. Just dump your wet stuff in the bathtub. Take your time. I'll be here waiting.'

The shower, so warm and so comforting, washed over Bianca. As the water streamed over her, she stood still and visualised her old life gurgling down the plug hole. With each drop of water part of her former life slipped away: the misery of living in that forsaken village – gone; the antagonism of her classmates – gone; the assault on her body by Mick – gone: the fear with which she had been living for the last few weeks, now washed away, swirling with the water down the plug hole and heading away from her – for ever. The taps turned off, for a moment Bianca paused in silent contemplation and then wrung the drips from her hair.

'Gone, all gone,' she tells herself. 'That was my past. Now I have a future and never again will I return to that rotten place.'

She expects that when she returns Penny will be full of questions and for a moment she is apprehensive as to what to say. But then she realises that for now all she need to do is convince Penny to let her stay – and that cannot be too hard, can it?

Well, a few tears seem to work wonders. For some reason Penny is easily convinced to let her stay the night or maybe a few days until she *feels recovered*. Reluctantly Bianca agrees that Penny can ring her parents to let them know she is safe and that she will stay in Sydney with Penny for a little while. Bianca is well aware that, as she has recently turned 18, her parents have little authority over her. So long as she is with Penny of her own free will and has not been abducted, there is little her parents can do. Any attempt to involve the authorities will be a waste of everyone's time.

As the days turn into weeks Bianca works hard to infiltrate herself into the very fabric of the daily activities of the house. She involves herself in the comings and goings of the students, replaces lost keys, collects and banks the rent and generally eases the workload for her godmother. With each day Penny relaxes into the idea of sharing her life with another. Someone to assume responsibility for the chaos that regularly ensues in the house, to greet her each evening when she returns exhausted from a day of lectures, and to cook an evening meal, with varying success: cooking never having been Bianca's strong point. On some evenings after surveying the latest failure, they both agree that a meal at the local Greek or Chinese cafes would more than do.

For her part Bianca delights in her new life. Sharing the house with the university students means there is always something happening. A party, a performance or a drama, as someone's heart is broken, or as a new romance commences. For a young woman who delights in change, every day's excitement is a new adventure and distracts Bianca from her lingering worries.

Bianca adapts to city living as if she was made for it. She delights in the idea that out on the street, no-one knows who she is or is even interested. Yet with her distinctive looks – the pale skin and the titian ringlets - she is soon recognised in the shops and cafes that line the nearby streets. Recognised for the local she now is, greeted with smiles and welcoming words, but not cross examined about her life. It is enough to say she lives with her godmother further down Glebe Point Road for her to divert any questioning.

During the day while Penny is at university and after a token tidy up each morning – after all there is only so much tidiness a girl can take, and it appears to Bianca that her godmother also suffers from domestic blindness – Bianca heads outside to continue her exploration of the city. The first week she focusses on understanding where in Glebe Penny's house is located and how to access the park by the harbour at the end of the road. For hours, she walks along the streets and alleyways in the suburb, delighting in the variety of architecture and the range of people out on the streets, all intent on their own business and paying her no mind.

The next week, having identified which bus heads in to the city, she catches it, and gazes out of the window with wonder as the bus travels into town, past the railway station to where she had only recently arrived, down George Street, past shops and arcades and then finally alighting at Circular Quay, where she gazes in awe at the harbour, a-jostle with ferries and boats. The Harbour Bridge towering before her and to her right the scar on the landscape of the Opera House, now well under construction. Across the harbour, the vista of even more buildings which all in all, combine to make her feel anonymous and insignificant. A very welcome feeling. After all the years of being known and tagged as the local doctor's weird daughter, being unknown and of no interest to passers-by was something to be celebrated.

That day when she was first deposited by the bus down by Circular Quay, Bianca walked towards the Rocks, an area she had only ever heard of in her history lessons. On and on she walked, right up to the approach to the Harbour Bridge, to the grassed area underneath the solid pylons where she sat contemplating the activity on the harbour. Pleasantly alone and solitary for some time until disturbed by a homeless man wanting to talk to her, she then stood and wandered away without acknowledging his presence. Losing herself in the Rocks she strode up the steep steps cut into the cliff until she reached another, higher level of terraces. That day she discovered if she just walked towards the direction of Glebe, sooner or later she would arrive back home. Skirting the west facing side of the city, traversing the hills in Pyrmont and dodging the traffic, she crossed the busy roads. It took a while but eventually she found herself back at Penny's house. That evening, an exhausted but triumphant Bianca bid an early goodnight to her godmother and headed up to her loft bedroom in the converted coach house out the back of the house. Lying back on her bed and in the brief few moments before sleep claimed her Bianca smiled contentedly. This new life is turning out just as she had hoped.

Chapter Seventeen

1975 – Penny and Bianca

Did Bianca really expect that her new life would continue to run so smoothly and that there would be no aspects of her old life to drag her back? It's possible that she thought she had left her past behind her. After all she was only just 18 and with limited life experience. It is also possible that, because she was so thin and had blocked out those recent traumatic events, any changes taking place in her body had escaped Bianca's notice. Or she might have just been in denial and was refusing to contemplate the reality that was fast looming into existence.

Penny, whose mind was so often focussed on times and people long ago, was slow to notice the changes happening to her goddaughter. Certainly, on that wet night when she opened the door to a sodden Bianca she had noticed her goddaughter was rather slim, almost skinny. At times in subsequent weeks she had congratulated herself that her focus in fattening up Bianca seemed to be working. It wasn't until Bianca had been in residence for about three months that the reality finally dawned on Penny. Watching Bianca shrug out of a sweatshirt, and as her t-shirt caught in the folds when the sweatshirt is dragged off, Penny stared in dawning horror as the neat swelling of Bianca's belly was momentarily revealed. What would have caused such a belly on such a slender frame is now all too obvious. Yet apparently not so obvious to Bianca, as Penny soon discovered.

'Bianca, when were you going to tell me about your baby?'

'What baby?'

'You're pregnant dear. Look at your belly. It's not fat.'

'Of course, it is. I've been eating for Australia since I arrived here. I told you that you were overfeeding me. I can't be pregnant. There's no way I could be pregnant! Oh…'

With an expression of disgust and a hand held over her mouth, Bianca stared back at her godmother. Clearly the realisation has now dawned that it is easily possible she could be pregnant. As her sex education classes at school had so often warned, it only takes one slip up for a pregnancy to occur. She was now living proof as to the accuracy of this warning.

'Oh, no. What am I to do?'

'Well, not panic for a start. That won't change things and certainly crying won't help. Here grab a tissue,' says Penny, proffering a dusty box of tissues that had been lurking hidden in the mess on the floor.

'I think the first thing to do is to see the doctor up the road, to confirm our suspicions that you are indeed pregnant and not harbouring some massive tumour.'

Bianca's hopeful look at the prospect of an alternative diagnosis clearly demonstrated to Penny that this is not a welcomed or hoped-for pregnancy.

A visit the next day to the local doctor confirmed their diagnosis. Bianca is indeed pregnant and possibly four months along. The doctor, a cheerful young man, failed to notice the strained expressions on both women's faces:

'Yes, indeed. Congratulations Bianca. You're well along. About four months I would say from my examination. You had no idea, you say? I suppose being so tiny you would not have shown for quite some time. But now it's clearly obvious. My nurse will assist you in giving you some information about pregnancy and you will be needing to go to some pre-natal classes. Otherwise you appear to be in perfect health. No issues with blood pressure and you are a fine age for your first child. I'll order some blood tests just to be safe, and then I don't need to see you for another month. You and your godmother may wish to think about the delivery – there are many options – home birth – not that I'd recommend that given your size and that it is a first baby. Or a birthing clinic – if you can get in that is – or the local hospital – with or without a specialist. A bit to think about, but we can discuss this further at your next visit once you have had time to do your research and I suppose start thinking about the future. A few things to get your head across I suppose.'

Penny ushers a clearly shaken Bianca out of the surgery.

'Come on. I think we both need a sugar hit – there's a cake shop just over the road. It's calling me and I would kill for a coffee.'

The cake shop, one of Bianca's favourites, is fuggy with the warmth of happy customers and fragrant with the scent of freshly baked bread. Penny orders for both of them, while Bianca bags two seats at the end of the counter looking out onto the street.

Penny, returning with a number on a stick clutched in her hand, settles into the seat with a sigh.

'Well I ordered us a pot of Earl Grey tea and I got the last two cinnamon scrolls.'

Looking anxiously at her goddaughter Penny continues: 'So my dear, are you OK? I'm sorry it's not a tumour. You must be the only person in this country who would be wishing for a tumour. But there it is. Your little tumour is really a baby, which will expel in about five months. Let me see – that means the due date is about January? Maths is not my strong point, but I think that might be right. Of course, if you knew when your baby was conceived then the calculations would be much simpler. You know about 40 weeks of pregnancy, more or less, from date of conception.'

Bianca's closed expression and hunched body language is a clear sign that even Penny can decipher. It is obvious that Bianca does not wish to share details about the conception – or even the baby.

Well, maybe there has been enough trauma for the day, Penny thinks. After all, Penny concludes the baby is not going anywhere and perhaps she should concentrate on cheering up her goddaughter. The timely arrival of food and cake and the necessity to pour tea and focus on eating provides a welcome distraction. They talk of this and that, but not the baby – anything but the baby. Yet as they talk, Penny observes that Bianca's left hand remains protectively on her belly and thus on her baby.

It's possible that all is not so hopeless after all, Penny thinks. But for the moment she keeps that thought to herself.

That the pregnancy was so advanced before it was discovered meant that the usual discussions about termination or not were no longer relevant, assuming that is, that a provider could be located. With the kindly encouragement of the midwife at the neo-natal classes and with the support of her GP, by the time she was seven months pregnant Bianca's ambivalence about the pregnancy began to fade. Almost without conscious thought she started to anticipate the arrival of her baby. It probably helped that with her dainty physique, vibrant red hair and alabaster skin, she presented as the archetypal mother-to-be. Glowing in good health and serenity she attracted admiring comments wherever she went. At the end of semester most of the students had vacated the house, leaving only the few who were staying over summer, for further study at summer school or having taken casual employment. These remaining students now took the opportunity to fuss over the pregnant one, almost as if they have adopted her as their team mascot.

From time to time Penny attempted to discuss with Bianca her plans for the future: whether she planned to return to *Kings Vale* or even if she planned to inform her parents about the pregnancy. Each time she is rebuffed. Bianca makes it very clear she has no intention of ever going home and that as far as she is concerned that part of her life is now over. But as to any future plans, assuming she has made some – well that is something she is not prepared to share with her godmother. Ever averse to conflict, Penny leaves it be.

For her part Bianca has no idea of what to do. For weeks she had been ignoring the changes in her body – the tenderness of her breasts and the occasional nausea, as if by willpower alone she could alter her destiny. Then came a day when she was no longer able to ignore the mocking of the ever-growing belly, which was forcing her to face up to the reality that would soon be her life. At first this changing belly was the focus of hatred and fury that she was stuck with the evidence of Mick's assault. Her dreams, populated with scenes of her giving birth to a tiny fully formed Mick, shocked her awake and filled Bianca with dread. Bianca had never been clucky. Indeed, she was still a child herself and found it hard to contemplate a situation where she would be responsible for another human being. Her sister's baby – that red-faced squalling brat filled her with revulsion and the thought that she would shortly have one of her own – leaking vomit and faeces, overwhelmed her with feelings of disgust.

Then things changed. It was almost as if the baby knew it had to fight back and win over the host mother. With timid fluttering's, the baby started to make its presence felt. At first Bianca didn't notice these movements or dismissed them as indigestion. Not interested in the baby and certainly not interested in the pregnancy, she had ignored those brochures the nursing sister had thrust upon her and so had no awareness of what was happening inside the sheltering cocoon of her body. Then those fluttering's became stronger, transforming into waves that rippled across her belly. With dawning wonder Bianca realised that what she felt gurgling inside her belonged to her baby who could create its own movements and in that way, already was independent of her. She could not control the start nor finish of these movements, although she did notice they were stronger each evening, when she lay down for a rest.

'Baby, what are you doing? Can't you let your mother rest? Or are you training me for the future?'

She found herself talking to this hidden being and with her hand rubbing her belly, she tracked the inner activity of her infant. Images of Mick faded, as she became aware of the new person that was growing inside her.

'You're your own person, aren't you? You don't belong to me and you certainly don't belong to him! You are you, unblemished and unspoilt by this world. I suppose I owe it to you to give you a chance and not blame you for your creation. You had no say in that – and neither did I for that matter. But here we are – maybe both victims, but I would rather think both survivors.'

One evening towards the end of the eighth month Penny broached the dreaded subject of the future. Each time she had tried to speak to Bianca about her plans for the future, she had been brushed off, but this time she was determined. Penny chose her opportunity with care. Dinner finished and tidied away, they were both relaxing before the television. In theory watching some dismal game show, but neither of them paying much attention. Watching Bianca absentmindedly rubbing her stomach, Penny seized her opportunity.

'Bianca, I know you don't like to talk about it, but it isn't long until your baby will be born and it's time to discuss what will happen next.'

'What do you mean?' Bianca's face is scrunched in puzzlement, as if she doesn't understand what is at issue. 'I'll have the baby.'

'Yes of course. But what I am asking is whether you have thought about the future. Will you keep the baby, or would you consider adopting it out?'

The look of horror on Bianca's face is a clear answer, but her words confirm her feelings.

'No Penny. Definitely not! How could I do that to my baby?'

'Be practical dear. How do you plan to support yourself and your baby? I'm happy to help you, of course. But you are still young and you may not wish to stay around a boring old person like me.'

'You're kidding me. Boring - you? And this house? I never know what drama will happen next! If you would let baby and me stay I promise I will do everything I can to help you run the house. You won't have to worry about anything. I'll keep the students under control - well as much as possible. Then you'll be free to focus on your work. If you are ok with having a squalling baby around, that is?'

'Of course. There is always a home for you here – if you want. You know, I never thought I would have a family. I let go of those dreams years ago when it was clear it was either career or family. This is going to be a new experience for both of us, but I'm rather excited about the changes – so long as you are sure?'

'I really wouldn't want to be anywhere else.'

Chapter Eighteen

1975 – Penny and Bianca

The experience of a Sydney summer came as a surprise to Bianca. Air like treacle, so thick with humidity that it exhausted her just to walk up the street to buy the groceries. The squally afternoon storms preceded by southerly changes were so different to the dry heat of the southern tablelands. Heavy and ponderous with child, her once flitting movements were now a distant memory. Bianca trapped in the reality of late pregnancy, found herself wondering if this was to ever be her lot – unable to bend or even to see her toes, which she had to hope were still there and in some sort of respectable state.

In the evenings she desperately wished for an end to this suffering, when, shiny with sweat, she tried to find a position of comfort on the now unsupportive bed.

'Come on baby. Time's up.'

The only answer, a sudden jab under her ribs and a poking hand or foot stretching through the skin of her belly. Bianca's hand tried to grab at the appendage, which retreated from her touch.

'Admit it. You can't be comfortable in there. You've outgrown your home. It's time.'

The doctor at the last examination also agreed with Bianca.

'Any day now. You are ready to go into labour. I can see your cervix has softened and things are about to happen. It's your first baby, so your labour might take a while. No need to panic at the first contraction. Just ring the hospital once they start to come regularly and be guided by them. You're young and healthy. I truly believe you will be fine. You may feel like this baby is a monster. But, for your petite build he or she is a nice size. If I was betting I think your baby would be about six pounds in the old language.'

Each morning Penny would reluctantly leave for work. Her anxiety about Bianca evident.

'Are you sure you will be ok? How do you feel? Any twinges? I can stay here if you wish?'

'No Penny – go. I am fine. Nothing is happening. Pity. Although I think I might make curry tonight and jump up and down to try and start something.'

'Don't you dare! Or at least not until I get home tonight.'

Maybe the baby overheard this conversation, but by late afternoon, as Bianca stood by the stove stirring the planned curry, she became aware of a dull ache spreading across the small of her back. An ache, something like the annoying period pain she used to experience each month. With each circle of the wooden spoon in the saucepan the pain nagged at her spine – now waxing – now waning. But bearable – a bit like an overture – a precursor to what was to come. But so far nothing to complain about.

Two hours later, as Penny let herself in through the leadlight front door, the ache had morphed into a monster. There in the kitchen was Bianca, no longer serenely stirring the curry, but with claw-like fingers clutching the edge of the kitchen bench, as she rode the waves of pain churning through her. A horrified Penny rushed to her side.

'Bianca. Why didn't you ring me? Have you spoken to the hospital? Are you timing the contractions?'

Through gritted teeth and as another contraction surges past, Bianca struggled to answer.

'No. I haven't rung. And no. I'm not timing – it seemed too soon – but maybe I now should?'

Another contraction hit and sucked all thought of speech from her head. Bianca, lost in the swirl of pain that is childbirth, felt herself falling into an abyss of torment. She had no awareness of Penny's strong arms guiding her to the family room couch, nor heard the concerned words being spoken over the phone.

'Yes, I've just got home, and things seem to have progressed rather quickly. I am timing the contractions now. Just the last two – and they're less than three minutes apart. I'm not sure what to do? Have we left it too late to drive to the hospital? Yes, I see – and here's another one. Definitely speeding up. An ambulance – would you be able to send one? Please stay on the line – she's saying she wants to push. What? Tell her not to? Oh, I see. Not too quickly or she might rip. Well, I'll try to distract her. I'm not sure I can. Can I see the baby's head crowning? Hold on.'

Penny leans over the now screaming Bianca and with soft words pries Bianca's legs apart and then speaks to whoever is on the phone.

'Yes. I can see a head appearing with each contraction and then receding. Can I feel around the neck of the baby? You're kidding me! I'm an academic and not a midwife! I don't think I can do that! OK, I get it. I'll try. She's pushing – I can't stop her. In fact, I don't think she can even stop herself. Here comes the head. What? Ease it out – I can't see the cord by the way – and ease the shoulders. Oh my god! We have a baby! Bianca – look your baby is here! What do I do now?'

By the time the ambulance team arrived some ten minutes later, mother and baby were cocooned in blankets and lying on the now bloody lounge. Baby, resting on Bianca's belly, and still attached to her mother by the cord. Penny showed the paramedics into the room then, with quivering legs, sat down. The shock of the recent events was now catching up with her as the room spun before her eyes. One paramedic glancing her way noticed Penny's distress.

'You did well Mrs. I think you have the makings of a paramedic. Are you OK? Just put your head down between your legs and take deep breaths. It's not often childbirth happens in your own home, but you didn't need us. You were a hero. As were mum and bub here.'

Turning to Bianca they first examined the baby's, then Bianca's vital signs. Satisfied that all was satisfactory the paramedics, clearly experienced in these events, applied themselves to the tying of the cord and the delivery of the placenta. A few more contractions and it was delivered in a bloody rush. Placenta captured and bagged for future examination, mother and child were eased onto a trolley and loaded into the ambulance, with Penny as an escort. Penny, seated by the now drowsy Bianca, patted her hand in reassurance.

'You were amazing Bianca. So brave and now you're a mother. A baby. A little girl by the way – well done you.'

'A girl?' Bianca's murmured response is barely discernible. Then with increasing energy as the message hits home, a smile splits her face, her happiness genuine.

'A girl? How amazing. We did it – and I tell you what – never ever again!'

'All mothers say that love,' the burly paramedic says. 'But she is a beauty. You've done well and your first. You're a trooper.'

Much later at the hospital, mother and daughter have been tidied up in fresh clothes: mother in a cotton nightie and tucked tightly in bed, daughter in hospital issue gown and now swaddled in cotton blanket, secure in her mother's arms. Penny sitting by the bed glows with pride.

'So much for our doctor saying it would take ages. Look at you - just popped her out in the kitchen. Like it has been done for hundreds of years. And almost by yourself too. If I had been delayed at work, I am sure you would have managed on your own.'

'Not sure about that Penny. I'm so glad you were there. No one ever told me it would hurt so much, but then how powerful I would feel. Like I was being swept along by a tsunami. The books don't mention that!'

'Maybe they're written by men or childless women like me! Never mind. You did well and now you need to rest. I think they're bringing you a cup of tea and some supper, and then you and bub need to sleep.'

With kisses and cuddles and promises to return first thing in the morning Penny gave a reluctant farewell to both mum and baby. Silence descended on the room and its inhabitants. Bianca, propped up in the bed, gazed down on the bundle in her arms.

Did this really happen? It feels all so surreal, she thinks to herself. Her trembling fingers tugged at the blanket to reveal the baby to inspecting eyes. The babe slept on.

'Welcome to the world, little one,' she whispers. Although why she is whispering Bianca doesn't know, as they are the only occupants in the hospital room. Perhaps it is the solemnity of the occasion or the fact that her voice is hoarse from screaming, but somehow whispering is all she can manage, or wants to do.

Cold air on the now unwrapped baby registers on newborn skin and she stirs. Eyes still shut, but little squeaks are now being emitted from pursed lips.

'Look at you,' murmurs Bianca while cupping the dainty head covered in golden fuzz, then stroking a downy soft cheek and running along a fragile arm towards the instinctively grasping fingers.

'Who would have thought I would be a mum? But there you are and here I am – a family – the two of us – well, maybe the three of us, if we include Penny, and of course we should. But what to call you? Nothing to remind me of the other family that's for sure – that's all behind us. Although a bit of a cultural reference might be fitting – but not Shakespeare – sorry Dad! Let me think. Why not Ariadne? I like that – its rhythm and the way it rolls of the tongue. Yes, that suits you. Ariadne for the thread that binds us together and will lead us both to our new home – not sure what home it will be, but I guess that is part of the mystery. Ariadne – I like it – but maybe for every day we can call you Ria. What do you think? Well, baby - what DO you think?'

As if in response, the baby's eyes open. So, like the eyes of her mother, but with that blurry unfocused look peculiar to all newborn babies, she gazes up at this face staring intently down at her. Name or no name it is of scant interest to this baby girl. Instinct tells her that food is on hand and with questing movements and sucking sounds she makes her needs known.

'I see. So, this is how it is to be. No more deep and meaningfuls. Just focus on food and then more food. Well, I suppose we had better get started. Let's just hope your mother can sort out how this breast-feeding works little girl. You'd better know what you're doing, as I certainly don't!'

Chapter Nineteen

2001 – Ria

Only two days back in Sydney and Ria had resumed her old life – well sort of. Rostered onto day shift at the hospital, she was up early and out of the house before Penny stirred. Upon her return each evening she would sweep into the bin the messages taken by whoever answered the phone. Messages recording countless phone calls from Geordie, each with a request that she return his call. As if! Even if he was the last person in the world there was no way she would ever talk to him again. Her hurt at his rejection firming into moral outrage that he could treat her so. Yet in her quieter moments, when her sensible inner voice could peep through, she would be reminded of Geordie's kindness and decency – how he had made her laugh and how, just one night spent with him, had made her realise there was nothing to be gained by being chaste. Resolutely she pushed those thoughts aside, although with each passing day it took more and more energy to do so. Still those phone messages were being left for her and still they ended up in the bin.

Every evening she pleaded tiredness and retired to her room as soon as she could after dinner. Alone in her bedroom she contemplated the misery that her life had become. Penny, well aware of the miasma of sorrow that trailed Ria wherever she went, did her best to leave her be, trusting that time would be a healer. Yet, after a few weeks of no apparent improvement, she lost patience. One evening as Ria pushed her chair away from the table to make her usual exit, Penny with a hand on Ria's arm, spoke:

'It's time we talked dear. You can't go on like this for much longer. If this isn't doing your head in, it's certainly doing mine! You'll be driving my guests away shortly with that long face. Come on – talk to me.'

Sad eyes contemplate Penny. Slumped shoulders speak more clearly than words. But still silence. Perhaps Ria has nothing to say? But Penny is made of strong stuff and doesn't give up that easily. After all this young woman is like the daughter she never had and is much beloved.

'I now regret giving you that letter. Yes, I know it was your mother's wish that you got to know what remains of your family, but they seem to have brought you nothing but grief – just like what happened to your mother. I wish I could take that letter back, but there it is – you met them. Things did not go as planned and maybe now we know why your mother ran away.'

'Not exactly,' Ria ever conscious of the need to speak accurately, finally engages with Penny.

'You see, I still don't know why mum ran away. I never got to ask and maybe I will never know. I'm beginning to realise that I just have to accept not knowing. I appreciate that you're trying to help Penny – really, I do - but I'm still struggling to understand why it ended the way it did. It all seemed so perfect – like it was meant to be, in that I'd met my family at last. Sorry Penny, that came out wrong – you're my family also and probably more so than them. After all you helped raise me and have always been there for me. I guess I should call them my blood family. At the start when I first arrived at the farm, it was all warm and friendly, and I felt like I'd found my perfect fit. The farm, the animals, my aunt and Ben were just so – so – I don't know how to say it – so right for me. Like I belonged. And then it all went wrong and turned into my worst nightmare. Doubly painful. It was as if I was having a dream snatched away from me for no logical reason.'

'Maybe we will understand why it happened in time, but I worry about you. Such sorrow, so soon after all the grief with your mother's illness and death. If I could help you I would, but I don't know how. I just wish you would speak to me.'

Penny's words make Ria feel even worse. So fixated had she been on her own suffering, that she had failed to appreciate the hurt she was inflicting on her beloved Penny. Her hand reaches across and sits on top of Penny's hand, which is still resting on Ria's other arm.

'I'm sorry. I've been very thoughtless.'

'Not thoughtless. Just a bit self-absorbed. That's perfectly understandable, after all that's happened to you, but bottling up your grief won't make the misery go away you know.'

'You're right there. I've already noticed that! I thought going back to work would help – you know by focusing on other people's troubles I would have a distraction. It hasn't. I just go through my days like an automaton. The matron thinks I am still grieving for mum – well I probably am. She's been so kind, but I think there's a limit to her patience. Today she asked me if I wanted to take more leave *to recover*. I think she is worried I might make a mistake and harm a patient.'

'I'm sure you're too professional for that. But maybe she is right about taking a break. Maybe you do need a change of scene. Go away somewhere? You know I've been thinking…'

'Thinking? This sounds like trouble. Spit it out.'

'That's more like you,' says Penny with a laugh. 'Yes, thinking. It's time I also had a change. I have been making some decisions. It's time I retired and had some fun before it's too late. I'm over 60 you know, and the years are speeding by. So, I wanted to talk to you about selling this house and buying something smaller, still with room for both of us, but not a BnB and not something that would tie me to one spot. I want to see those historical sites I have been lecturing about for all these years. I know this is your childhood home and that's why I needed to check if what I am planning is ok with you. You'll always have a home with me – if you still want one that is….' Penny's voice trails off as she looks anxiously at Ria, looking almost as if she is uncertain about the response.

Ria exhales and leans back into her chair, all thought of retiring to her room now forgotten. As she stares at Penny in amazement, she notices the newly visible streaks of grey in her wiry cropped hair. For so long Penny had been vibrant and energetically focussed on her career. To hear her calmly contemplate a future away from the university seemed so alien to the Penny she thought she knew. If her beloved, almost relative could contemplate creating a new life, then why couldn't she?

'Penny, that came out of left field. I would never have expected this. What an adventure! And you don't have to worry about how I would feel if you sell this house. It's your house after all. You grew up here, just like me, and if you are able to move on, then so can I. Although if there is room for me in your new home – well – I'd kind of like that. You're the only family I have after all.'

'No. Don't you play the victim on me! Just because the relatives behaved badly that is no reason to disown them. Listen to me – accept that your experience of family is limited, so your expectations might have been formed based on fairy tales and not on reality. Family can be messy and complicated. Give it time and keep an open mind. That open mind is really important now – as something came for you in today's post. Now where did I put it?'

After some searching and much muttering Penny finally locates an envelope and hands it over. Ria holds the letter in both hands – turning it over and squinting at the scrawled address of the sender.

'It's from *Kings View*. From my aunt.'

Still no attempt to open it. She just stares blankly at Penny.

'Well, it won't open itself you know. Go on – your aunt has taken the trouble to write to you. So, read it.'

Letter eased from envelope, unfolded and read in silence – except for one snort. Penny, desperate to know what has been written, squirms impatiently in her seat. After some moments, during which Ria gives no reaction as to the effect of the letter on her, Penny succumbs to the tension and interrupts Ria's silent contemplation of the pages before her.

'Well? What does she say? Anything helpful? Put me out of my misery please.'

'It's a sort of an apology. I think that's what it is. Listen,' and Ria slowly reads the letter out aloud:

Dear Ria

I'm sorry it's taken me so long to write this letter. I hope that by now you are home and settled into your Sydney life. Ben tells me I treated you badly and I suppose I have.

With another snort, Ria adds a comment: 'See what I mean – a sort of apology,' and then she continues reading to Penny.

I don't expect you to understand why I behaved as I did in sending you away so suddenly, but as a mother I felt it my priority to settle Kitty and take away all things that were causing her stress. And one of those things was you.

I hope in time life will become calmer and Kitty will be much more reasonable. It was a pleasure having you here – well it was for me – and also for Ben. We miss you and hope that one day you can visit again.

With love

Your aunt.

'I still don't get it,' says Ria as she slowly folds the letter and replaces it in the envelope. 'Why wouldn't my aunt be more assertive and pull her daughter into line when she was being a cow? Or just plain rude – meaning no disrespect to cows. But the question is still why – why did Kat behave as she did?'

'Not being a mum, I can't say. But I can guess. Kitty had returned home unexpectedly after such a long time away – who knows where – and maybe Kat didn't want to risk her running away again? You know she'd lost her husband and her daughter and was doing her best to hold the farming business together. The return of Kitty must have felt like an opportunity to rebuild her family and create a new future. Although from what you've said about your cousin Kitty she doesn't sound like the best sort of material with which to create a solid family life. Still your aunt seems to be trying her hardest. Question is whether Kitty really intends to linger, or is she just being there 'cause it suits her for the time being?'

'You know, when I think about it and all the unpleasantness that lurked below the surface once Kitty returned to the farm, maybe it is a good thing that I'm far away. I'm not going to write back though. How can I when all I will want to do is tell her how much they've hurt me?'

'Like I said, families can be messy and complicated. Your aunt is holding out the hope that one day you will be able to visit again. Hold onto that thought. And while we are talking – well I don't mean to interfere - but don't you think it is time you returned the calls from that young gentleman? If he had really meant to dump you I'm sure he wouldn't be spending so much energy ringing you every day. From what you told me when you first met him he sounds like he is a decent sort of man. Don't forget we all stuff things up from time to time. Don't you think you should give him a chance to explain?'

Ria's frown makes it very clear that she is not going to be drawn into any discussion concerning Geordie. She stands and heads for the door.

'You're right Penny. You shouldn't interfere. Just leave it. I do not intend to speak to him again. There's no point.'

That night as Ria gets ready for bed, she continues to dwell on the words in her aunt's letter.

They miss me – well, Aunt Kat and Ben that is. I'm sure Kitty is so glad I'm gone and she now gets all the attention. And Geordie? What to do with him? It's such a mess. Was I too mean to him at the railway station? Should I have been more understanding? After all what he was saying made perfect sense – it is very hard to maintain a long-distance relationship and we had barely a relationship anyway. But it was just the last thing I wanted to hear after being rejected by Aunt Kat. Then being rejected by Geordie – that just compounded the hurt. Maybe he is calling to say he misses me? And I certainly miss him. But I just don't think I can talk to him – not yet.

Chapter Twenty

With the passing of time, the pain that had been impacting on Ria's life lessened. It didn't go away completely, as so much had contributed to her devastation. Not a day went by when she didn't think of her mother – when using her mum's favourite coffee mug, watering her pot plants in the courtyard or wishing to share with her an amusing work anecdote. Having seen the way Kitty related to her mother, Ria had come to appreciate that the relationship she had shared with her own mother was special. Their love was something she had taken for granted, but in hindsight she could see it was something she should treasure and maybe, one day, use as a template for any other loving relationship.

On her evening shifts at the hospital there were quiet moments when all the patients were asleep, and she had the opportunity to catch up on the paperwork and enjoy a coffee. Sitting at the ward desk, paperwork now done, Ria would find her thoughts drifting back to those days at *Kings View*, as she tried to make sense of what had actually occurred. With the receding of her anguish, Ria came to appreciate that perhaps the excessive hurt she had felt was because she had invested too much hope into this new life. Had her mother's illness and death made her vulnerable, so much so, that even without conscious thought she had been susceptible to what was in fact a fantasy? Yet when she thought of the shared laughter with Ben, the magic that was Tonka and the joy found in everyday life on the farm, Ria was still convinced that so much of what she had experienced had been real and had resonated with her very being.

These midnight ponderings did not alter the dull ache that still accompanied Ria in her daily life. Yet they served a purpose. The more she pondered, the more she felt certain that Sydney was no longer for her.

I have a skill I can use anywhere. Why stay here where the noise, smog and hassle of daily living makes everything a battle? If nothing else, my stay at Kings View has taught me that I love the countryside - so what am I waiting for?

That evening, over an early dinner and before leaving for work, Ria shared her plans with Penny.

'What an excellent idea. It's time you spread your wings. Don't forget, that apart from your recent adventure, this is the only life you've ever known. If you do make your plans that will give me incentive to get off my bum and put this house on the market. Who knows, we might be able to sell it as an ongoing BnB. It's got to be an attractive proposition based on the forward bookings. Then I can sort myself out. I've already told the uni I'm leaving at the end of this academic year – which is fast approaching.'

Taking a deep breath and smiling at her favourite person, Penny continued, 'You know Ria this could be the making of us both. Your mum would be so proud. Bianca always loved change. In my mind's eye I can see her here at the table crowing with excitement, taking over and making all the arrangements for us. It's time my dear that we both moved on with our lives – starting tomorrow!'

Later, when she contemplated the changes wrought by the following days and weeks, Ria wondered if the reason she was now ready to engage so fully in them was because of that conversation with her Penny. That somehow her mind had already decided for her life was going to change and so made it easier for her to accept an invitation which, weeks ago when she was in such an emotional quagmire, she would have rejected outright.

The next day was again a workday and Ria was pottering around the house doing the usual chores, prior to leaving in the evening for the last of her night shifts.

So, pleased to be back on day shifts next week. Night shifts are a killer – in more ways than one,' she thought to herself. *'Why is it when things go wrong during the night shift, they always go wrong so catastrophically?*

Still pondering this and the challenges of the previous night's shift, when the phone rang she casually reached for the earpiece and answered, not really paying close attention. The screeching at the other end jolted her into the present and full awareness. Where had she heard such a screech before?

Screeching's morphing into incomprehensible sobbing sounds. Ria, holding the phone away from her head, pondered who it could be. Then the voice changed, and an immediately recognisable voice came on line. Returning the handset to her ear, Ria now listened:

'Hi cuz. It's Ben. Sorry about that. Kitty insisted on phoning you, but she's just a bit emotional and you probably couldn't understand what she was saying?'

'You're right there. I had no idea who it was – although the sound was vaguely familiar. Why are you calling? I'm late for work, so please keep it quick.'

Ben's voice – so unexpected and so welcome – yet Ria knew she could not let down her defences and let him know how happy she felt just hearing him speak. Not yet anyway. Not until she knew whether she was about to be blamed for something else.

'I get it. You're not sure what you're in for. I understand. We treated you so badly and there really is no reason to ever speak to us again. But Ria it's not like that – really. I know we kinda mucked it up, but I so much want to make amends. Kitty and mum have had a bit of time to consider their behaviour and – well – what Kitty was trying to say was ...'

His voice is interrupted mid-sentence and Kitty comes back on line. Ria can only assume that Kitty has snatched the receiver from Ben's hand. Ria can hear a 'What the… Give it back Kitty,' in the background as Kitty, a now somewhat less emotional Kitty, starts to speak.

'Ria, it's me, Kitty. What Ben is trying to say is that I'm sorry – so sorry. I was mean to you and I want us to be friends. I really do. I hope you can forgive me – and I need you – please can you get down here. I've had the baby and I can't cope. You, with all your nursing experience will know what to do. I promise I will be good. I can be you know. Please I beg you – anyway don't you want to see the baby?'

'The baby? You've had the baby already?'

'Yeah. I was a kinda wrong with my dates – probably about two weeks out. It was a bit of a surprise and a rush to get to the hospital on time. But it all went ok, and I now have a daughter. She's about ten days old and it's a bit much. She doesn't sleep. I don't sleep and I'm still sore and leaking – everywhere! Mum and Ben do what they can, but they have so much else to do on the farm – it's awful,' and with that the agonised sobs resume. Ben comes back on line.

'See what I mean. Humans with babies are much more trouble than animal mothers. Come on. You want to see what your new cousin looks like – and hey, Tonka misses you. He's getting so fat being turned out in the paddock with no exercise. When can you get here? This time I'll be on time to collect you from the station – promise!'

Despite her best intentions Ria smiles and finds herself agreeing to see what she can do.

'I have to talk to work, mind you. I can't just drop everything and rush back. It's not that simple, but I'll see if I can get some more leave in a week or so. You'll just have to manage until then. Try and let Kitty get some rest. It's so much easier to cope with most things after a decent sleep.'

'Will do.'

'Are you sure your mother wants me back? It was pretty clear last time that she wanted me gone and away from Kitty.'

'Who do you think suggested to Kitty that she ring you? She wants you back. In fact, I think she wants you here for her own purposes –

not just for Kitty. With Shelley gone, she is barely managing with the function business – it's wedding season after all. Norma helps – well, sort of. At her age Norma isn't much help for anything. Remember Norma? – our old farm managers widow and was once dad's nanny? She lives in one of the cottages down by the creek. She does her best but we need you, the miracle worker! Go on – aren't you tempted?'

With assurances that she will speak to her boss tomorrow and see if she can get leave, Ria ends the call just as Penny enters the room. In response to Penny's quizzical look Ria explains:

'You'll never guess! That was a call from Kitty and Ben. It's almost so unbelievable that I wonder if I should be suspicious. They want me back. Do you think they just want me back to yell at me again? Maybe I shouldn't go.'

'Don't play the victim Ria. There isn't always a hidden motive or an unhappy ending. What else did they say?'

'Just that Kitty has had her baby – about ten days ago. She had a daughter. Strange she didn't mention her name. I hope it's not another weird name inflicted on an unsuspecting mite. Anyway, Kitty said she is barely managing, and Ben seemed to agree with that. I suppose that she can't cope should come as no surprise. The impression I got when I was there was that Kitty could barely look after herself – so caring for a baby might be beyond her.' Ria draws a breath and looking thoughtful, continues. 'You know I'm tempted – I would love to see the baby, and Ben and Tonka.' (*and maybe Geordie if I'm brave enough,* she thinks.) 'But what if it turns out like last time? I'm not sure I have the strength to deal with that.'

'You're doing it again. Overthinking things my dear. Why worry about things that may never happen? Did they sound genuine?'

Replaying the conversation in her head, Ria nods.

'Yes, I think so and they said my aunt suggested they call.'

'Then do it. What have you got to lose? This time forget the romantic idea of happy families and just engage with them as they really are. Warts and all, and I don't mean that literally. They do sound like people just trying to make the best of difficult circumstances – like the rest of us. Don't forget they have yet to get to know the real you. The one who forgets the time of day when she has her head in a book, who can burn a dinner without even trying, just like her mother, and who is the most loving young woman I know.'

'Penny. What would I do without you? You're so wise' smiles Ria, giving her not quite family member a quick hug, before her face clouds over as she continues. 'I'm not sure I am brave enough to face them again. Part of me wants to – but I just don't know if I can face all that angst again.'

'Wait a minute.' Penny's voice is stern. 'You are the person who deals with life and death on an almost daily basis and you're telling me you're not brave enough. Give me a break! Listen to me girl. Listen to your elders. This story is not yet finished. You need to go back and pick off that scab. The hurt, the wound that was inflicted last time, needs to be revisited and healed. After all, with your career as a nurse, your entire mission is to heal. So, do what you do best – just go there and heal yourself – and if you are lucky maybe you can sort out the rest of them. I'm right you know. Promise me you'll think about it?'

'Yeah. You're probably right. You usually are,' concedes Ria with a grin. 'I'll think about it. Must dash now or I will be late for work.'

With a further hug, a smile and a wave she leaves the room, not noticing Penny's crossed fingers.

For once the night shift goes smoothly. With no emergency late night admissions and no catastrophes affecting her young patients, Ria has plenty of time to consider Penny's words.

Maybe Penny is correct. I do need to go back and discover one way or the other, whether there is a future for me with that family and perhaps even with that man. For my own peace of mind, I need to know.

Somehow she knew that the Ria, about to embark on this journey was a different woman to the one that sat apprehensively in the railway carriage all those months ago.

This time she would get it right.

Chapter Twenty-One

This time the trip to *Kings Vale* was a known journey. No longer any need to peer anxiously at the signs as they arrived at each station, she could relax and admire the passing scenery. Everywhere she looked there were signs that spring was unfurling. Peering through the window Ria admired the paddocks, like emerald velvet dotted with white puff balls of sheep surrounded by lambs or black cows and calves. All arrayed for her entertainment – so much so, that she had no need to read the book that lay neglected in her lap.

With each mile travelled, quivering feelings of anticipation grew. Unlike the Ria of that last journey to *Kings Vale*, when she had been awash with grief and fatigue, now her body trembled with excitement. So much of what was waiting for her she loved and somehow, she knew that this time she could find the inner strength to manage those challenging bits.

But then, alighting from the railway carriage onto the platform at *Kings Vale* and seeing who was waiting for her, Ria felt the courage draining away from her. Maybe she was not quite ready for this?

Standing on that dusty railway platform was a young man waiting, watching as she tentatively approached, dragging a suitcase behind her. But not the young man she had expected. With his close cropped wiry dark hair and tall muscular frame, she knew exactly who he was. After all, hadn't she last seen him on this very same platform, when he had left her speechless and heartbroken?

It was Geordie. Standing still and observing her approach. His felt farm hat being twisted out of shape by agitated hands. So, he was nervous, was he? Just as well - maybe that thought gave Ria some encouragement, for she found she could manage to greet him with a taut smile and a hug – just. Then the feel of his firm body as she put her arms around him, and the smell of his clean skin did something to the logic of her thinking. All she wanted to do was stand still, holding and smelling and willing time to slow down – just for a few more moments. And maybe to see if the kisses she had tried so hard to forget, were as perfect as she recalled in those sleepless nights. Perhaps Geordie also felt the same way, for his arms tightened, then lifted her off the ground.

'Welcome home Ria,' he said then followed with a quick peck on the cheek. Geordie set her down and stepped back a tentative smile on his face. Was he really that uncertain about his reception?

'Why are you here? Is Ben OK? I thought he was going to meet me?'

'He was, but then he suggested that I come in his place. He thought we might need to talk – sort things out. There's a new café in the village – does a decent coffee. Fancy checking it out?'

'Sure, but just a quick coffee. My aunt will be expecting me.'

The café, picture perfect, in a renovated worker's cottage, just along the street from the pub, was full of gossiping people. A table located on the front porch and with orders given, they sat, both staring with concentration through tangled wisteria blossoms onto the street. Staring as if there was something of great interest out there. Like that night when they left the pub, they were silent as if uncertain what to say and then, both started to speak at once.

'Sorry,' said Geordie. 'You go first.'

'No, you.' Ria having immediately decided that she needed to hear what he had to say. What Geordie said and how he said it, she knew would influence her response.

'Alright then. I suppose I needed to clear the air. You know last time we spoke I said what I said because – this is the hard bit – I said that because I didn't want to be a burden on you. You were already so upset from your aunt's behaviour, and I didn't want you to feel like you were beholden to me in any way. But somehow it came out wrong and I think you might have misinterpreted it.'

'Well, the meaning was pretty clear. You said you wanted a break – or words like that.'

'Not very tactful, I know. But words aren't my strong point. I'm a simple farmer don't forget – not sophisticated, like you city folk. If I could take those words back I would – but can I update them?'

A dimple makes a fleeting appearance, along with an expectant look.

Ever the sucker for dimples, she smiles. Maybe she does want to hear what is about to be said.

'An update sounds fine. After all it has been a few months since your last statement and maybe it needs revision – hopefully for the better and not like my current bank statement. Go on then. I'm listening.'

'This is starting to sound like some fancy business meeting. But if you want to keep it formal so be it. Madam Chairman, what I am proposing is we start again. That we wipe the slate clean of all previous transactions and commence our negotiations from the very beginning.'

'ALL previous transactions?'

That dimple again.

'I see what you mean. Some of them could count as market research and, depending on changes in the market, we might want to conduct further investigations?'

Eyes engage and focus on each other – blue gazing into those of deepening amber. No words said as the moment extends and hands reach out across the table.

'You're on,' exclaims Ria. 'I just love a business proposition. So romantic! After all, it is very important that we focus on our due diligence – no dodgy deals here! Starting immediately, I assume?'

'Too right!'

The drive home seemed to take longer than last time, with Geordie insisting on driving past the dirt road turn off that headed to *Kings View* so he could show Ria where his family farm was located. It wasn't far away. Just a little bit further along the sealed bitumen road. Geordie explained that his family's farm shared a boundary with *Kings View* where the back boundary of both properties met. He turned into the front gates but didn't drive up the driveway.

'I'll bring you here when we have a bit more time and I can show you around properly. Maybe meet the parents – if you're up for it that is. They're not scary – just desperate for me to have a girlfriend. I hope that doesn't put you off?'

'Could be interesting. Maybe they have some stories to tell me about why they're so desperate?'

'Then again – maybe I should keep you lot apart?' He laughs and turns the car around to head back in the direction from where they came. Back to the turn off up the dirt road. Up the hill, potholes just as Ria remembered.

'Doesn't anyone ever repair this road?'

'Not often,' comes the laconic reply. 'Why bother, when it all gets washed out again at the next rain.'

Down the hill and across the rattly bridge. A feeling of familiarity washes over Ria and with it brings a contentment as if she was returning to a place that sang to her very being.

This does feel right, she thinks. *Like I belong here. I just hope the others feel the same way.*

This time the car does not stop at the front door. Geordie turns off the driveway before reaching the house and parks down by the side of the building, next to a path that leads to the kitchen. Ria takes her time getting out of the car. Suddenly feeling apprehensive she stands still, pretending to gaze outwards across the garden, all the while trying to gather sufficient courage to walk up to the kitchen door. A hand at her elbow and with a gentle push Geordie encourages her forward.

'Come on. You can do this. I'm pretty sure it will not be as bad as you expect. Trust me.'

How did he know what I was thinking? she wonders silently. *Am I that obvious?*

'No, you're not. Just we farmers are very good at reading body language. This way – the only way is forward. You riders should know that!'

He opens the screen door and ushers her into the kitchen. Three faces look up and then with cheers they leap up to greet her, followed by a small bouncing white dog.

'At last. Come here my girl. Just ignore that dog.' Aunt Kat swarms forward and wraps Ria with welcoming arms. 'It's about time – we've been waiting for ages. I suppose Geordie took you the long way home? Welcome home my dear. We have some bubbles on ice and I thought seeing as the afternoon is so warm we might go outside into the courtyard. Never mind me,' the last words said to Ben, who unceremoniously pushes in demanding a hug.

'What about me?' This time an indignant Kitty squeezes herself into what is now a group hug by four people.

'Hey, give the poor girl some air. You'll scare her off and then where will we be?' laughs Geordie. In a chaos of laughter, chatter and high-pitched barking no-one pays him any attention. Geordie smiles and shrugs. He goes to locate the glasses and the bubbly and leaves them to it.

A little while later all five people are settled on the benches outside. Sparkling wine now poured into elegant long-stemmed glasses and held up high by each person, as Ben proposes a toast.

'Here's to our gorgeous Ria who cannot keep away, no matter how awful we are to her! No seriously, it's wonderful to have you back with us and this time, we will never let you get away – even if I have to chain you to this here oak tree!' In response to a glare from Kitty, he continues 'Oh yeah. And here's to my gorgeous, yet to be named niece and her exhausted mother. Go sister!'

Anxiously Ria looks around. Where is this mysterious baby?

'She's asleep – finally. You'll meet her soon enough. This baby doesn't sleep for very long – unfortunately,' says Kitty.

Now that they are all seated Ria has the opportunity to examine Kitty and her aunt. Both slumped on the bench, faces drained and wan, they look like people in need of rest.

'It's been pretty full on has it?' she asks trying to convey with a sympathetic look how she understands what they have been going through.

'That's an understatement!' exclaims Kitty. 'This is definitely an only child. Not that I'd even planned it.'

'Her,' you mean corrects Kitty's mother, who then continues, 'and yes, it has been full on. Wedding season has started, which on its own is a full-time job, but on top of that we also have this little one to care for as well. Norma lends a hand when she can – and you will meet Norma shortly. She and the baby are in the lounge room watching the tv – or Norma is. Although she could be asleep. I don't know how we'd manage without her.' Perhaps feeling uncertain as to whether Ria is following the conversation she adds: 'Norma was my husband's nanny all those years ago and she gave me a hand as well when the children were little. She probably thought her nannying days were long over, but I guess you never forget and we are so grateful she can still pitch in and help.'

'Have you got a name yet?' Ria is curious as to what name this family, with a taste for unusual names, would choose. Mother, daughter and son exchange exasperated looks. Kitty grumbles.

'No, we haven't,' she says. 'Not for want of trying. You see I don't want to inflict an awful name on her, but it's too hard. Picking a name is so final. What if it doesn't suit her when she gets older?'

'So what? She can always change it,' says Ben. 'You can't call her *she* or *it* or *baby* for the rest of her life. Call her after one or other of our grandmothers or an ancestor or something out of the newspaper or your favourite tv soapie for the matter. Anything – or I'll give her a name. It can't be that hard, can it? After all I find names for the horses and the dogs quite easily,' he concludes, not so modestly.

Kitty bristles in indignation.

'I will not call my baby after one of your horses – or after your dog for that matter.'

'Why not? Bess is a good name. And she is an excellent sheep dog.'

Before full scale warfare erupts, Aunt Kat intervenes and calms her two children – one of whom is looking daggers at the other, who is laughing at his own excellent wit.

'You two. Stop it now! What will Ria think?'

'It's OK Aunt Kat. Now I feel like I'm back in your home – squabbling siblings and all that – something I never had growing up and sometimes I missed it - but not often.'

The sound of a door opening and closing, then Ria can see a woman walking along the enclosed veranda with a bundle in her arms. Out through the door and into the courtyard. All heads turn to contemplate her approach. It is the woman Ria had occasionally seen at a distance last time she had visited. This must be the mysterious Norma, the widow of a former farm hand who lives in a cottage down by the creek. Her age indeterminate – but clearly old if she had once been nanny to Ria's uncle. With short grey curly hair and rounded rosy cheeks, she has the appearance of a friendly fairy book granny. A pink floral ruffled apron belted around her waist and a towel over her shoulder complete the look of domestic reliability. Ria's eyes take all this in as she watches Norma approach and then her gaze falls onto the bundle in Norma's arms. So tiny. Yet this was something Ria was accustomed to in her role as paediatric nurse. Tiny and snuffling.

'Oh, no. Not again. I only fed her an hour or so ago. Surely not. It hurts so,' says Kitty standing up and moving towards Norma. 'Here, give her to me. I'll go and feed her. Sorry everyone. It's too hard to do in front of you all. Back soon,' and with bundle in hand Kitty returns inside, followed by Norma who mutters something about seeing to dinner.

In response to Ria's querying look, her aunt opens up, sharing details of the last few weeks. The drama of Kitty's premature labour, the rushed and panicked trip to hospital, forty minutes' drive away, their arrival just in time and the delivery of a perfect little girl. Dainty like her mother with the same reddish golden hair – although at this stage only discernible as a fuzz over a delicately shaped head. The family tradition of blue eyes passed onto another generation.

'In fact,' says her aunt, 'the baby is a mirror image of her mother, which is just as well, as we have no idea who the father is. Chances are that neither does Kitty.'

Seeing Ria's puzzled look Ben interrupts and explains.

'She won't talk about it much, but from what she's told me Kitty was living it pretty rough on the streets. Selling drugs and herself - whilst she hasn't told me much exactly - I suspect Kitty did whatever she could to survive. Still she's clean for now and the baby is healthy. The team at the hospital did their checks and were quite definite about that. It's just – mum and baby are both pretty unsettled, and that means we all need to help. Maybe you might have some ideas of what to do?'

All eyes turn to her expectantly and Ria now feels the weight of family expectation – as if she could save the situation with little effort. With a non-committal 'I'll see what is possible,' she changes the topic to divert them into discussion on other matters. It works. Soon her aunt is chattering on about the next wedding – to be held in two days' time and talks about the burden of owning so popular a wedding venue.

Ben adds his bit – waxing lyrical about the amazing spring season, with its abundance of growth in the paddocks. He and Geordie soon descend into technical discussion about lambing and calving successes and failures, why some things went wrong and how to improve for next year. Totally focussed on their conversation. So boring!

Kat takes Ria by the hand and pulls her up.

'Let's leave these old farmers to their bonding. Walk with me. Let me show you the spring flowers. The blossom and the bulbs are still out. I hope they last until the weekend for the wedding.'

She leads Ria around the courtyard, having tucked her niece's hand firmly in the crook of her arm. Tubs of multi-coloured tulips that line the courtyard are duly admired. The just opening wisteria along the outside of the enclosed veranda commented on.

'Planted by my mother-in-law you know. It is so vigorous and would take over the house if it could, but it is a saviour in summer when it blocks out the late afternoon sun. Yes, it will be still out this weekend – then next week you will be on the leaf blower, just like last time. The spent wisteria falls everywhere and becomes a carpet of dangerous slime if we aren't vigilant. Beauty followed by danger – a metaphor for life I suppose.' She laughs, 'Don't mind me. I must have drunk too much – I'm getting way too deep. Come on dear – this way.'

They leave the courtyard and turn towards the front of the house, heading across the gravelled front driveway towards the gardens that enclose the tennis court. The buzz of bees working the grouped blossom trees before them.

'I just love these crab apple trees – so hardy yet rewarding. Look at how beautiful they are in spring and then in autumn they will be equally lovely, when the leaves are every shade from orange through to burgundy and covered in so many tiny crab apples, which will attract the parrots. My favourite trees – although that changes week by week, as something else comes into bloom. And just look at these peonies here. So lush, you'd swear they were fake.'

A bed of peonies in shades of pink and mauve duly smelt and admired, they turn, still arm in arm meandering in the general direction of the house.

Ria can sense her aunt's unease by the way her hand tightens on Ria's arm and has a fair idea of what her aunt is about to say before she starts. Clearing her throat Aunt Kat launches into a rushed speech:

'I owe you an apology Ria. I am really sorry and should never have treated you the way I did. It was so unfair on you, the innocent party. I just wanted Kitty to be at home and happy and yet every day we were on tenterhooks. That morning I overreacted and sent you away before I could cool down. Ben was furious with me and I deserved it. I didn't think of the hurt I was inflicting on you. All I was thinking about was the need to get you away from here and hoping that would change things. Of course, it didn't. The problem is Kitty and her personality. You being here or not, didn't change things in the slightest. I'm really grateful you have come back and given us a second chance. We don't really deserve it. I just hope this time we can make it up to you.'

Aunt and niece pause and gaze deeply into each other's eyes. Whatever they see appears to be mutually satisfactory as with a smile, a hug and a kiss, they laugh and then resume their perambulations back towards the house.

A clanging of a gong and a yell from Ben indicates dinner is ready, that he is starving and will eat their share if they don't hurry.

Later that evening Ria lies in her bed and contemplates the activities of the day. No longer given the run of the cottage, which she has been informed is reserved for wedding guests and the occasional farm stay tourist, she is now in occupation of a bedroom in the main house. A guest room at that and some distance from the family bedrooms, but still, she hopes an indication of being one step closer to being included in this family. The room located upstairs above the kitchen, along with several other unoccupied rooms, is furnished in what Ria would describe as shabby country chic. Furnished some time ago, the floral linen weave curtains that drape the large window show signs of fading by the sun. When she pulls the curtains closed she can see the original colour running dark lines of flowers down the fabric, where they have been hidden for so long in the creases away from the light. The double brass bed topped with a patchwork quilt is surprisingly comfortable. Ria gives thanks that the mattress is not of the same vintage as the bed and the rest of the furnishings. The adjoining bathroom is positively Victorian in its size and fittings. With a clawfoot bath in pride of place in the centre, the room looks chilly and so uninviting in the cool of the evening. The floral decorated porcelain toilet bowl with pull cord hanging from an overhead cistern surprises her by actually working. The feeling of being on the set of some costume drama had returned earlier that evening when, pushing her unpacked suitcase under the brass bed, she had surprised an enormous ceramic chamber pot. Fortunately, empty.

Lying back on the firm bed, the quilt pulled up close, she ponders her return. The family so welcoming, it is as if the events of those months ago had never happened. Norma and Geordie's presence at dinner and with the flow of general conversation and gossip, there had been no time for a proper conversation with Ben. She hoped that when they went for a ride first thing next morning he might be more revealing. With a smile she recalled the attention that Geordie paid her over dinner. Insisting on sitting next to her and making sure she had plenty of helpings of the beef lasagne that Norma had prepared.

The discussions at dinner had been lively and far ranging. She now feels like she has caught up with the local gossip and the goings on with the farm. A particular discussion she recalls with a smile. At one stage, when all were speculating on the baby's future name Kitty took strenuous objection to Ben referring to her as *no name*.

'You can't call her that – she is a person and deserves to be treated with respect.'

'Well, give her a name then. It can't be that hard. Here let me help you.' Grabbing a pen and pad of writing paper from the mess at the end of the table, he looked at Kitty.

'I propose a ballot. Tell me the names and I'll put them in this hat here. Geordie pass me your hat. You can pull out a name and hey presto, we will have a decision and then the poor baby's birth can be registered, so she can be treated like a real person at last. Sound like a plan? I think it's a pretty good one myself,' says Ben, modest as always.

Kitty concedes defeat.

'OK then. Let me see.' She pauses, scrunches up her face as if in deep and painful thought and then continues 'But I don't really like many names.'

'Well what about our grandmother's names?'

'Mum's mum is ok. She was Olivia Kate. I like that. But dad's mum Beryl Elsie. No way!'

'I quite like Elsie,' Aunt Kat muses. 'A good strong name – after all you need to be strong to be in this family.'

Silence descends, as they all contemplate the significance of this comment.

'What about favourite movie stars?' Geordie asks, by way of distraction.

'I quite like Julia – you know Julia Roberts and maybe Sarah – like Sarah Jessica Parker. But I don't know – none of them seem right. Ria – your mum? I know she was called Bianca but what was her middle name.'

'Her middle name was Sophia – not that I ever heard her mention that. I only know for sure, as her full name was printed out on the death certificate.'

'That's right,' says Aunt Kat. 'Bianca Sophia – Sophia meaning wisdom I think. Dad was really into symbolism and Shakespeare with our names. Though I think Sophia is from the Greek?'

'I like it,' says Kitty, speaking slowly as she ponders the name. 'Sophia, Sophie for short – for everyday – it's a name with attitude. Not too fancy and owing nothing to Shakespeare. Wisdom – you say. Well, she'll need plenty of that living with us. Forget about the hat Ben – it won't be needed and anyway, it's a silly idea. Sophia, it is. Mum are you ok if her middle name is Kate? Sophia Kate Kingsley. The perfect name for a future Prime Minister – a real lady, but not one to be messed with.'

Raising their glasses and smiles of relief all around they propose a toast to the no longer nameless baby.

'Good one sis – so glad that's finally sorted. More trouble than naming my dogs,' says Ben. 'Now can we have dessert?'

The creamy tiramisu that followed was perfect. Several hours later and lying replete on her bed, hands settled on the bump of her stomach, Ria felt just shy of overfull. Another mouthful would have tipped her over. Thank goodness Ben had snatched the dish from her with his greedy hands or she would be regretting it now.

Thoughts reverting back to Geordie, Ria acknowledged the vague feelings of regret that he had left so soon after dinner. She had walked him out to his car. With a lingering kiss or two or more and a cuddle with intent, he promised to return the next night and take her out *to dinner or somewhere.*

Surveying the relative privacy of her new sleeping quarters – accessible via the steep stairs just off the front entrance and so far from curious relatives – she speculated whether this location might be a mutually acceptable *or somewhere* for them to visit tomorrow night.'

So long as Kitty had no further disruptive plans. Of that Ria was not completely sure, although she suspected that Kitty was currently too exhausted to worry about anything other than sleep. She had excused herself from the table soon after dessert was completed, but not before Ben with a laugh in his voice, accused her of shirking washing up duties.

Handing the sleeping baby over to Ria and with a mumbled 'whatever' in Ben's direction, Kitty had wandered off towards the bedrooms, the sound of continuous yawning trailing behind her.

With a smile Ria remembered her first close encounter with young Sophie – who by her calculations was her cousin once removed. Such a proper label for this small, slightly damp bundle. Ever efficient in all things, she had immediately set to work, using the small change table set up in the corner of the adjoining lounge room. A perfect opportunity to inspect this little person, now stirring as the cool evening air impacted on her uncovered body. What Ria could observe was a slightly underweight baby with long limbs, hinting at the potential to exceed her mother's height once she had grown up. Wide awake, the baby peered solemnly up at this new face from large eyes framed by impossibly dark lashes.

'You lucky girl. Dark lashes and I suppose with time, those stray hairs there on your forehead, will become dark eyebrows. Unlike me, you will not be consigned to a lifetime of mascara application. Must be due to your father I suspect, as we are all a family of sandy eyelashes. Some more sandy than others.'

The baby stares back solemnly, listened intently to this strange new voice and giving the appearance of someone fascinated by beauty tips.

Now changed, wrapped up, warm and dry, the baby wriggled and squirmed, cheek turning as she looked for sustenance. Clearly not an unanticipated occurrence, for when Ria returned to the kitchen her aunt handed her a bottle.

'Here you go. We've been supplementing her for a while now, but I think we should just take the plunge and put her on the bottle full time. She's not getting enough from Kitty. I think in part that might be the reason for her restlessness. Poor little mite is just plain hungry.'

Conversation then ceased as all adults in the room focused on the feeding of young Sophie, lying securely in Ria's arms. As a nurse Ria knew exactly what to do and before long the fully sated baby was resting upright – head resting on Ria's shoulder and emitting satisfactory burps until eyes rolling back into her head she relaxed into a fully contented sleep.

I think Sophie had the right idea. Dinner and then sleep. Maybe she can teach me a thing or two about priorities.

With that thought in mind and with a smile Ria rolled over. Like her newborn cousin, she then succumbed to blissful unconsciousness.

Chapter Twenty-Two

Next morning Ria was up early and out in the kitchen waiting impatiently for Ben to appear - her excited anticipation of a horse ride on her beloved Tonka a far greater attraction than the prospect of any sleep in. The early spring air, still chill but with promise of a fine sunny day ahead. All she wanted to do was be outside. Nevertheless, she urged herself to be patient and busied herself with making a cup of tea and toast, while she waited for Ben.

If he doesn't appear soon, so help me, I'll go and wake him myself. If only I knew which bedroom was his.

Just as Ria was summonsing up her courage to investigate the bedrooms down the other wing that abutted the courtyard, she heard the sound of a toilet flushing, a door opening, and a rather bedraggled Ben appeared. Eyes still bleary with sleep and with hair tangled in all directions, he was not a thing of beauty.

'You really don't give bedroom hair a good name, do you?'

'Good morning to you, little cousin. Remind me again why I missed you and where's my cup of tea?'

'Here's one I prepared earlier,' she said handing over a still steaming mug. 'And some toast. Then can we go – please?'

'Relax. The horses aren't going anywhere without us. Let me wake up.'

But Ria is off, out into the back porch, where she has located a pair of riding boots that looked like they will fit. Boots now on and with some stamping to check for comfort, she calls for Ben.

'Come on. Bring your toast. Let's get going before the others wake up and change our plans.'

'Good point. I'm there.'

With toast hanging out of his mouth and mug in hand, Ben joined her and they were soon wandering along the dewy path towards the stables. Not much conversation given Ben's toasty impediment, but Ria didn't mind. The morning's beauty more than compensated for the lack of scintillating repartee from her cousin. Watery beads of dew caught on spiderwebs captured the light. Dampness brushed their faces as they walked through the webs some industrious spiders had woven across the path in the night.

'Ugh,' splutters Ben. 'I didn't need that. Looks like Bess will be getting this toast, spider's web and all.' He whistled for his dog, who had raced ahead. With tongue lolling and mouth wide open almost like a grin, she bolted back to her master in anticipation of her treat.

The horses heard their noise. Heads raised they contemplated their approach. All glossy with spring condition and artfully arranged in groupings in the paddock, they could be posing as part of a photo shoot in praise of country living. The arranged serenity of the shot immediately dispelled, when Tonka in response to Ria's shout, whinnied and set off in full gallop to circuit the paddock – a mare and foal at his heels with all the other horses in close pursuit.

'Looks like they're full of beans this morning,' muttered Ben. 'We could be in for it. Sure, about this?'

'Never surer. Fancy that. You're trying to wimp out?'

'It's a dare, is it? Come on then – first to saddle up wins – first stage that is, and then – leave it to me – I'll think up another challenge.'

A carrot secreted in Ria's pocket immediately gives her a winning edge. Tonka enticed into the yard by means of bribery, she is well into saddling him up while Ben is still chasing Fidget around the paddock. Eventually caught and saddled both prancing horses with their riders head out up the laneway.

'So, you won that time. Let's see who gets to the end of the laneway first,' challenged Ben with a confident grin, and with a slight squeeze of his legs Fidget is off, leaving Tonka and his rider struggling to catch up.

By the time a breathless Ria catches up to a triumphant Ben, it is clear who has won.

'That is so not fair. Your horse is naturally faster and my poor old boy cannot run for that long, even if he was a bit fitter. Still that was fun.' Her glowing eyes and happy smile provide added emphasis.

'Yeah it was fun. I've missed our rides together. No fun racing yourself. It just doesn't work. I think we should take it slowly home. Our poor horses – look at how puffed they are. Before we do so though let's go up the hill and check out the view. You haven't been up there since late summer.'

Horses, still puffing, leisurely wander at loose rein up the rise. Just like last time, when halted by their riders, they take the opportunity to snatch at the lush spring grass in the paddock. All around them, the paddocks are a vision of green – in shades from light green where freshly mown, to dark emerald in the paddocks that are being spelled. In the distance, the village is mostly hidden from sight by the newly unfurled foliage on stately deciduous trees.

Ria makes what she hopes are suitably acceptable admiring noises, for in reality she is at a loss to explain how moved she is by the beauty of this wide expanse in every shade of green that had once been in her childhood set of colouring in pencils. She recalls how delighted she was to receive that set one Christmas and how amazed that there could be so many different shades of green in existence. At the time she had wondered how she would ever be able to use them all in one picture. Finally, many years later, here in front of her, the practical application of those colours has been clearly demonstrated. Yet, whatever she has said seemed to satisfy Ben. Muttering something about needing to get back and help out with the chores, he turned Fidget around and headed down the hill. Ria followed – reluctantly – for she would much rather linger outside enjoying the beauty of the day in the company of her cousin and the obliging horses, than doing any chores associated with yet another wedding. From her previous experience she expected that such chores will involve weeding or polishing – or both.

When they finally arrive back at the house, sweaty and smelling of horse, they find the household in a state of uproar. Norma, standing and holding a crying baby, while a sobbing Aunt Kat sits crumpled on the chair at the table. Ben enters the kitchen first and is immediately set upon by his mother, who hurls herself into his arms.

'Ben. It's too awful. I don't know what to do,' she wailed.

'Steady,' he said, trying to pat her on the back. With eyebrows raised he looked over his mother to Norma and asked, 'what's happened? Are you OK?'

Norma shrugs but says nothing. Taking his mother by the hand and leading her to the settee that is over by the side wall, he sits them both down, all the while murmuring quietly.

'Deep breaths now. Take your time. Ria can you put the kettle on? I think mum could do with a cup of tea and I suspect we all could – or maybe it should be something stronger? And Norma, can you make that baby stop crying?'

'I think she might need a bottle,' says Ria. 'I'll sort that out as well. Perhaps Norma, while I do that, would you please take Sophie outside? That might distract her. Just for a minute. I'll get the bottle warmed as soon as I can.'

Norma gives Ria a grateful smile and takes the still crying baby outside.

'There, now we can hear ourselves think,' says Ben. 'Come on mum. Out with it.'

Aunt Kat looked helplessly into Ben's eyes and in a shuddering voice she starts to speak.

'It's Kitty,' she says and then stops.

'Kitty?' asks Ben. 'Has she hurt herself?'

'No. No. Not that, or at least, I don't think so. She's gone. Sometime before I got up. She's taken my little car, but she says she will leave it at the station.'

'So, you've spoken to her?'

'No – if I had maybe I could've convinced her to stay. She left a note – see on the table,' says Aunt Kat, her voice becoming fainter and more tremulous as the emotion washes over her. No more words to be said. She is beyond words and has once more succumbed to tears. Ria hands her a handkerchief and then returns to her task of tea making and heating the baby formula.

The letter located on the table; Ben starts to read out loud:

> *Sorry mum. But I just can't do this anymore. You know living here on the farm does my head in and now this ~~baby~~ Sophie – it's too much. I just have to get away and have some time to myself. I will keep in touch this time and maybe come back for a visit – never to live – sorry. I just can't do it. And I'm no good for the ~~baby~~ oops I mean Sophie. You, Norma and even Ria are much better mothers than I ever can be. It's not that I don't love her but I can't be responsible for another person. I can barely look after myself as it is.*

Ben pauses and looks up. 'I'm not sure what the next bit says – looks like Kitty was crying, as the ink is all blotchy. But there's not much else anyway. The last bit is legible:'

> *Mum I've taken your car to the station. Will leave it there unlocked and with the keys behind the visor. I'll ring you once I'm in Sydney. Believe me this is for the best – for all of us.*
>
> *Love you*
>
> *Kitty xxxx*

For a moment they are all silent. No more sounds of crying from Kat or from the baby outside. Then, with a cough Ben clears his throat, and takes charge:

'Ma, I know this is awful. You do know though that it comes as no surprise. She hates it here and maybe it's better Kitty has gone and left the baby …ummm …Sophie here with us. She can't give any child a stable life, when she herself is all over the shop. Let's hope, that in time she might sort herself out. At least we know Kitty is safe and I'm sure she'll keep her promise to stay in contact. Maybe when she does we can convince her to get some help – counselling or something. Think about it – that's an improvement on last time.'

'You may be right, Ben dear,' his mother speaks slowly, as if marshalling many different competing thoughts. 'I had hoped that when she returned this time Kitty had matured and grown away from the demons that haunted her. There was that set back when she heard about her father's death, but even so she seemed to be able to process it and what's weird, maybe she even welcomed it – like she was dreading seeing him again. I suppose that's not surprising after how they fought. Then again she also hates the farm - and rural living of course.'

Turning to face Ria who was now standing nearby she adds, 'In a way Kitty's just like your mother, who couldn't wait to get away. Maybe it is a family thing? You either love it or hate it here.' Her spare hand reaches for Ria. 'I'm so glad you have returned though. I had hoped you and Kitty would start anew. Obviously, that won't happen now. But maybe one day …' Her voice trails away.

They all look up, disturbed by the sounds of Norma returning through the door with a whimpering bundle.

'She's pretty desperate for a feed now. Ria, would you?'

Baby handed over, bottle produced and peace descends.

The rest of the day goes slowly. As if by unspoken consent, all planned chores are abandoned leaving the family to take comfort in the presence of each other, taking turns to cuddle the small baby and then to fight over whose turn it is to give Sophie her next bottle. Sophie, oblivious to the drama that surrounds her, snuggles into whichever set of comforting arms embrace her, while squinting up in puzzlement at the procession of faces that take turns in peering down at her: the faces of her family.

Geordie, arriving late afternoon, finds a strangely subdued family. Upon hearing the explanation his first reaction is to check on Kat's wellbeing. Ria, watching from a distance smiles thoughtfully. *Clearly this man is a keeper. He cares*, she thinks.

It wasn't as if Kitty had contributed much to the running of the household, the farm or the function business, but somehow her absence meant that the workload had increased significantly. That evening Aunt Kat, back in charge and focussing on the future, called a family meeting after dinner. *Family* she made it clear, also included Geordie – something that Ria couldn't help but appreciate.

'Now everyone. Pay attention,' spoke Aunt Kat, tapping the side of her wine glass with her fork.

'Careful with your wine glass mum,' says Ben. 'Don't spill the wine. It's a good drop.'

'Silly boy. Have you ever known me to waste my drink? Now listen. We have a lot to do the next few weeks and I think we need to sort out some sort of work programme. Ben, I suppose your work on the farm will continue as normal, but I expect you'll be wanting some sort of break to work on your latest sculpture. I'm not sure how we're going to be able to help you there, as I will need Ria with me. Perhaps Geordie?'

'It's OK mum. You and Ria worry about the functions. I'll help you where I can on the day, but I can't help you much in advance. The farm is pretty settled at the moment. Calving and lambing long gone and marking completed. A few weeks until we start the bulk of the hay making. Early grass cutting all done and turned into silage for winter. We're looking good. I do want to start on my next sculpture though. I might call it *Changes* – another one in my series on family life.'

His eyes lit up with excitement and with waving arms, Ben sketched the vision that was forming in his imagination. 'It's all a bit vague at this stage, but I'm envisaging a central curved shape which could symbolise our baby and maybe other curves unfurling somehow – protecting but moving away from the centre. Could be a disaster – often is with my work – yet I'd like a few days to work on the concept, before I forget it.'

The responsibility for Sophia provokes much discussion. Norma had already indicated she was happy to help with Kitty's baby whenever necessary. Perhaps, Ria speculated, the role of nanny was one she was happy to resume? Aunt Kat volunteered to take young Sophie with her each evening – as 'that is what I have already been doing for the last few weeks anyway,' with Ria on standby, if it all got too much. Ria could take care of Sophie during the times when Norma was not around – mornings and evenings and any other time she was needed. It was a very loose arrangement, but all agreed it was as much as they needed to agree for now and indeed was as much as they had the energy to organise.

That night they all retired for bed early: Aunt Kat pleading emotional exhaustion left first, wheeling Sophia, asleep in the enormous white cane pram, a relic from times long ago and followed by her fluffy white dog shadow. Ben then leaving the room, sketchpad in hand, overcome with inspiration and in no mood to waste time talking to others. Ria bidding them all goodnight, poured her and Geordie another glass of wine.

'I've got an idea.'

'Mmmm?' says Geordie taking another appreciative mouthful of wine. 'This red is really something.'

'Never mind that. I've something to show you. Bring your glass with you if you must. If you can't bear to leave it behind, that is. This way.'

Geordie followed Ria out of the kitchen, out onto the glassed-in veranda where they headed towards the entry foyer.

'Up here.' Ria pointed up the narrow stairs that opened off the foyer.

'I've never been up here. Where are you taking me woman?' he asked, the raised eyebrows giving clue to his expectations.

'You'll see. I think you will be pleasantly surprised.'

His one free arm reached for Ria before she could ascend the stairs, pulled her close and proceeded to make it clear what his intentions were.

That night they discovered that brass beds do not make for discrete lovemaking. With every movement, thrust and repositioning, the bed accompanied them with its running commentary of rattles and bangs.

'So glad no one else is sleeping nearby,' giggled Ria. 'With all this noise it sounds like we are holding an orgy up here.'

'Now there's an idea,' said by Geordie with a smirk.

'As if! Think you are up to it, do you? You farmers. Surrounded by bulls and their harems, it must be giving you ideas!'

Later, much later as they drift off to sleep, Geordie spooning into her back with one arm lying across her belly, Ria looked out across the room as she contemplated the new life that appeared to be overtaking her. No need to make a decision about whether to stay or leave. It looks like that decision has been made for her – by her aunt and by one very small baby. They both need her. As the arm tightens and as she feels a soft kiss planted on her shoulder, she smiles. Sometimes it is best to forget about decisions and just go with the flow.

Chapter Twenty-Three

With each passing day Ria finds herself settling into this new life. The first few days were hard, as she tried her best to support her aunt through her grief. Then Aunt Kat's stoicism came to the fore. At times in a brusque voice she would brush Ria's concern aside with dismissive words and then, usually by late in the day, she would weaken and confide in Ria how hard it was to keep going.

'You know I thought I had dealt with the worst after Mick died. I thought things couldn't get any grimmer – but then Kitty's leaving us just as I thought she was back for good. Well, I really feel like I have failed and I just have to accept that I cannot bring her back.'

As if becoming aware of Ria's concern, she continues, 'It's alright dear. Maybe it's part of getting older, but I am starting to understand that I cannot change people. I couldn't relieve Mick of his distress and I cannot change Kitty into the sort of person who would be happy living here.' Her eyes move to the small person lying on the padded quilt on the floor with nappy removed and kicking vigorously, as if in celebration about the lack of restraint.

'It's not all bad of course. Young Sophia is a delight. Now we have sorted out her feeding regime she has become the happiest and most settled soul. It's a shame that Kitty is missing out on seeing her daughter grow and I try not to dwell on that. I just take lots of photos and post them to her! I try to hold onto the thought that things will improve in time. After all Kitty has kept in contact as she promised and has given us her address – I should not give up hope. And you too dear. You came back to us, even though I would totally understand if you had washed your hands of us,' she says smiling into the eyes of her niece. 'I couldn't manage without you. Helping with the baby and the functions. I just hope I'm not placing too big a burden on you?'

Ria feels indignant. After all her aunt has gone through, there is no way she should be worrying about her niece.

'Not at all Aunt Kat. You've given me a home and I just love it here. All those years growing up in Sydney it never dawned on me that another way to live exists. It's been a bit of a challenge working up the courage to tell Penny I'm not coming back, but I rang her last night and she was fine – almost like she was not surprised. She says the house is sold and she will pack my stuff up and send it down. Only trouble is – are you sure you want me here? You know, I would totally understand if you think it might be too troublesome having me here – what with Kitty and all.'

Now her words are out in the open, Ria suddenly feels apprehensive. Maybe she has assumed she would be welcome to stay on a more permanent basis and that is not the case?

With loving arms her aunt pulls her in. 'Don't be ridiculous child. You belong. No doubt about that! But enough of that - I need to get moving.' Her tone reverts to her usual no-nonsense manner as Aunt Kat leaves the emotion behind. 'If I can leave you to sort out young Sophia there, I will give some thought to what there is to cook for dinner.'

Another evening, another family meal. This evening, Norma joins them as she often does. Ria suspects she is lonely down there in the cottage by herself. It could be that the added attraction of a gurgling baby entices her to linger for as long as possible. That evening, they eat their dinner whilst playing pass the baby. Sophie, now grown into her limbs and presenting with a healthy covering of firm flesh on arms and legs, is a comfortingly solid baby to cuddle. The golden down on her head is transforming into soft waves of a colour, very similar to the colour of Ria's hair – a reddish golden hue.

'You know,' says Ben, observing his niece interacting with a cooing Ria. 'She could almost be mistaken for your daughter. There's a strong family resemblance, what with that colouring and shape of face.'

'Not only that,' laughs Ria. 'Only the other day I discovered Sophie also has my birthmark. See that one on the back of her neck,' she says, pointing to the red splotch at the base of the baby's neck, which with a bit of creative imagination, could be seen to resemble a child's drawing of Australia. Pulling her hair up from her own neck Ria continues: 'and I also have a birthmark, in exactly the same position on my neck and from memory it is a similar shape.'

'Let me see.' Ben examines and agrees. 'Yep, they're identical, and a bit like mine as well. I think you're right. It must be a family thing. Kitty has one as I recall.' He looks up and notices the strange looks on both his mother's and Norma's faces.

'What did I say? Why're you looking at me like that?'

Like a Mexican standoff for some moments all four adults sit silently – two staring with puzzled questions on their face and a dawning realisation transforming the faces of the other two. Meanwhile Sophie, lost in her own conversation, continues with her babble.

'Well, that explains it,' says Norma at last. Kat nods with deliberation, like a judge having been convinced by some complicated legal argument.

'Explains what?' asks a clearly puzzled Ben.

Norma raises her eyebrows as if in question to Kat. A sort of *shall I tell them, or will you?*

'It's pretty simple really and rather obvious too when I think about it, but I didn't put 2 and 2 together. I should've, but there you go.'

'Mum. You're not talking sense,' says Ben again, but this time said in a sterner voice.

'You're right. The birthmark is a family thing and it does run down the generations. But in your father's family, not in mine. When I first saw you Ria I'd wondered – especially when I saw how alike you and Kitty are – and even Ben, come to that. But I'd other things on my mind, so I let it drop. Of course, I'd had my suspicions all those years ago, but I'd tried to ignore it.'

In growing apprehension Ria finds herself asking what is rapidly becoming evident.

'Are you telling me that I'm related to Ben and Kitty through more than just by our mothers being sisters?'

'I think so. I had my suspicions but didn't realise you also had the birthmark because of your long hair. It's possible that my husband Mick was your father. I don't know for sure, but the birthmark is fairly persuasive evidence to me – and I can tell that it convinces Norma too.'

She looks across at Norma who gives a nod. Kat continues, 'You see when your mother ran away all those years ago, I thought it fairly odd that Mick didn't react like the rest of us. We were so worried at that time and he just said to let her go as she was a spoilt little brat. Over the years he would shut down any conversation about Bianca, almost as if he felt uncomfortable about her name ever being mentioned. When we heard from Penny that you'd been born, he didn't want to know. And when Penny sent us photos of you, which she did from time to time, he'd leave the room rather than look at them. I didn't press him about it – well, I'd learnt very early on that you didn't press him about anything if you didn't want to be yelled at. He could be a very difficult man.'

'You're not wrong there,' agrees Ben.

'Then when Kitty ran away, he said a strange thing,' Kat says. 'He was devastated and really withdrew into himself. But one night he said something like: *I'm being punished.* Yet when I tried to find out what he meant by those words, he told me to shut up and that was the end of that.'

The identity of her father had never been of any concern to Ria. Her mother, Bianca and Penny, who filled the role of a sort of grandmother, had been all she had ever needed. If she ever contemplated the identity of a father, it had been as some nameless and faceless one-night stand. A person whose only use had been the donation of that life-giving sperm. But now she realised, with dawning horror the father who most likely brought her into existence was the man who featured in so many photos in this house. The implications of this were rapidly becoming clear. If she was Mick's daughter, how could she expect her aunt to tolerate her existence in this family? Again, she felt overwhelmed by the feeling of her happiness once more being snatched away from her.

Clasping Sophie close for what she knew could be one last hug, Ria spoke: 'I'm so sorry Aunt Kat. I don't know how he or mum could do this to you. But I understand I can't stay here – that would be way too inappropriate.'

'Steady on,' Ben jumped in before anyone else could speak. 'No need to overreact. Mum tell her. Tell Ria she belongs here. Now we know why she settled in so quickly. Sure, she's that old bastard's daughter – but hey she's family and she's my sister. We can't let her go. I can't lose another sister. That would be plain careless. Mum? Mum? Don't just sit there. Say something!' Ben ended his sentence on an almost pleading note as he looked anxiously across to his mother.

As if rousing herself from a contemplation so profound it was impossible to leave, Kat looked across to Norma in silent communication. It was only when she observed the silent communion between the two women did Ria realise how close these two are.

Before Kat can say anything, Norma spoke – enunciating each word with care and with emotion:

'So, Kat, we have just had confirmed something that both you and I had long suspected. That is all – a bit more of the puzzle fits – yet nothing has changed. Ria is still your niece and it seems to me completely unaware of her past. I suppose Bianca did that on purpose to protect her and as far as I can see there is no reason to punish her for something that happened so long ago. She is still Ria and you, my dear Kat, are still you. Both, if I may say so are people who have the ability to rise above anything that may have happened all those years ago. I've been witness to way too much heartbreak in this family and believe me, I don't want to see any more. Ben, it's not often I think you say anything that makes sense, but this time I agree with you.'

They all sit in silence waiting for Kat to say something – anything. She looked at them one by one, eyes glassy with unspilt tears and then contemplated the cooing infant so relaxed in her cousin/aunt's arms. Taking a deep breath Kat spoke:

'Norma, you are so wise, and Ben, you are right. I've lost a sister and maybe a daughter. Also, a husband, who despite all that has happened, I loved. I can't lose another member in this very dysfunctional family. Ria, dear I completely understand that it's not your fault who was your father – just like this little baby here, whose own father is still a mystery. Blame, if any, for your conception, sits with the parents – and as the true story is now lost to us, then I guess we will never know. At the time I had my suspicions and maybe that's why I let contact with your mum slip. Don't get me wrong – if I dwelled on all the things that had gone wrong in my past I would be a total wreck. At some stage I had to make the decision to look forward and refuse to be hurt by those I love. I don't want to punish you for something that has nothing to do with you. Ben's right. Not that I ever thought I would say that! You belong here – in this family, in whatever classification you choose to be. My sister's child, my stepdaughter or just plain Ria.'

Kat sighed, 'It's going to take us all a while to process this change, but you know what? I feel like a burden has lifted already! No more secrets! You're still the same person you were five minutes ago and it seems instinctively wrong to punish you for something you had no hand in. What we've discovered confirms what I suspected anyway, so it should not be a big deal. Who would have thought some good might come from such heartbreak? Maybe this might just guide us all when raising our Sophie. You belong to all of us, Ria dear, as does this little one.'

'Hey, good one mum,' smiled Ben, 'I knew you had it in you, my amazing mum.' With that he swept his mother in his arms and planted a kiss on her cheek.

Tears, laughter and more tears occupy that evening. Emotions run high, as does relief for some, that the truth has finally been made known.

New Beginnings

Neck and neck, they race down the laneway. Horses beside themselves in the excitement of an unchecked canter. Strides lengthening as they are urged on by their laughing riders. Through the open gate and into the far paddock. Horses now moving into a gallop as they charge up the hill, until the crest is reached. Restraining hands urge the horses to slow, which short of breath, they do.

'I won!' shouts Ria, cheeks aglow and eyes full of life.

'No, I won,' disputes Ben.

'Ridiculous boy! You're so wrong. My horse was clearly ahead. Your eyes definitely need testing!'

'No, Ria I won, and maybe you also won?' This time Ben speaks more slowly, emotion sparking in his eyes as he reaches out his hand.

'You see, I won another sister. And that is something special as far as I can see. Maybe you also won – 'cause you now have a brother. But perhaps - precious only child that you once were – maybe sharing a family – especially this family – isn't your idea of a prize?'

For a moment, he looks anxiously at her, doubt in his expression.

'Silly. Finding my family – no matter how imperfect is the best prize of all!'

About The Author

I have always loved telling stories but as a mother, a practising lawyer and counsellor I never had any time to write. A move to Tasmania gave me the opportunity to start a new career as an author.

My husband and I (as well as dogs, cats, chooks, cows and horses) live on a historic property in rural Tasmania. I draw on my farming background and legal and counselling experience for inspiration.

I have self-published a number of stories on Amazon Kindle and have published *Past Presence, Perfect Breaks* and *Sabine* in paperback through Publicious Publishing.

www.ingramcontent.com/pod-product-compliance
Lightning Source LLC
Chambersburg PA
CBHW032117020726
47494CB00007BA/2122